THE GRACIE ALLEN MURDER CASE

THE GRACIE ALLEN MURDER CASE

S. S. Van Dine

FELONY & MAYHEM PRESS • NEW YORK

All the characters and events portrayed in this work are fictitious.

THE GRACIE ALLEN MURDER CASE

A Felony & Mayhem mystery

PRINTING HISTORY
First edition (Scribner's): 1938

Felony & Mayhem edition: 2021

ISBN: 978-1-63194-206-8

Manufactured in the United States of America

Cataloging-in-Publication information for this book
is available from the Library of Congress

One never rises so high as when one does
not know where one is going.
—*Cromwell*

CHARACTERS OF THE BOOK

PHILO VANCE

JOHN F.-X. MARKHAM — *District Attorney of New York County*

ERNEST HEATH — *Sergeant of the Homicide Bureau*

GRACIE ALLEN — *A worker in a perfume factory*

GEORGE BURNS — *A perfume mixer and scent-tester*

DANIEL MIRCHE — *Maître d'hôtel of the Domdaniel café*

DIXIE DEL MARR — *Singer at the Domdaniel café*

C. AMOS DOOLSON — *President of the In-O-Scent Corporation*

JIMMY PUTTLE — *A perfume salesman*

MRS. ALLEN — *Gracie Allen's mother*

PHILIP ALLEN — *Gracie Allen's brother*

"OWL" OWEN — *Head of a large criminal ring*

BENNY THE BUZZARD (BENIAMINO PELLINZI) — *A gangster*

DELPHA (ROSA TOFANA) — *A fortune-teller*

TONY TOFANA — *Her husband*

SNITKIN

HENNESSEY

SULLIVAN

GUILFOYLE } *Detectives of the Homicide Bureau*

BURKE

EMERY

TRACY

DOCTOR EMANUEL DOREMUS   *Medical Examiner*

DOCTOR MENDEL   *Assistant Medical Examiner*

CURRIE   *Vance's valet*

The icon above says you're holding a copy of a book in the Felony & Mayhem "Vintage" category. These books were originally published prior to about 1965, and feature the kind of twisty, ingenious puzzles beloved by fans of Agatha Christie and John Dickson Carr. If you enjoy this book, you may well like other "Vintage" titles from Felony & Mayhem Press.

—◆—

For more about these books, and other Felony & Mayhem titles, or to place an order, please visit our website at:

www.FelonyAndMayhem.com

THE GRACIE ALLEN MURDER CASE

CHAPTER ONE

A Buzzard Escapes
(Friday, May 17; 8 p.m.)

PHILO VANCE, CURIOUSLY enough, always liked the
Gracie Allen murder case more than any of the others in which
he participated.

The case was, perhaps, not as serious as some of the
others—although, on second thought, I am not so sure that
this is strictly true. Indeed, it was fraught with many ominous
potentialities; and its basic elements (as I look back now)
were, in fact, intensely dramatic and sinister, despite its almost
constant leaven of humor.

I have often asked Vance why he felt so keen a fondness for
this case, and he has always airily retorted with a brief explana-
tion that it constituted his one patent failure as an investigator
of the many crimes presented to him by District Attorney John
F.-X. Markham.

"No—oh, no, Van; it was not *my* case at all, don't y' know," Vance drawled, as we sat before his grate fire one wintry evening, long after the events. "Really, y' know, I deserve none of the credit. I would have been utterly baffled and helpless had it not been for the charming Gracie Allen who always popped up at just the crucial moment to save me from disaster... If ever you should embalm the case in print, please place the credit where it rightfully belongs... My word, what an astonishing girl! The goddesses of Zeus' Olympian ménage never harassed old Priam and Agamemnon with the éclat exhibited by Gracie Allen in harassing the recidivists of that highly scented affair. Amazin'!..."

It was an almost unbelievable case from many angles, exceedingly unorthodox and unpredictable. The mystery and enchantment of perfume permeated the entire picture. The magic of fortune-telling and commercial haruspicy in general were intimately involved in its deciphering. And there was a human romantic element which lent it an unusual roseate color.

To start with, it was spring—the 17th day of May—and the weather was unusually mild. Vance and Markham and I had dined on the spacious veranda of the Bellwood Country Club, overlooking the Hudson. The three of us had chatted in desultory fashion, for this was to be an hour of sheer relaxation and pleasure, without any intrusion of the jarring criminal interludes which had, in recent years, marked so many of our talks.

However, even at this moment of serenity, ugly criminal angles were beginning to protrude, though unsuspected by any of us; and their shadow was creeping silently toward us.

We had finished our coffee and were sipping our *chartreuse* when Sergeant Heath,[*] looking grim and bewildered, appeared at the door leading from the main dining room to the veranda, and strode quickly to our table.

---

[*]   *Sergeant Ernest Heath, of the Homicide Bureau, who had been in charge of other cases which Vance had investigated.*

"Hello, Mr. Vance." His tone was hurried. "...Howdy, Chief. Sorry to bother you, but this came into the office half an hour after you left and, knowing where you were, I thought it best to bring it to you *pronto.*" He drew a folded yellow paper from his pocket and, opening it out, placed it emphatically before the District Attorney.

Markham read it carefully, shrugged his shoulders, and handed the paper back to Heath.

"I can't see," he said without emotion, "why this routine information should necessitate a trip up here."

Heath's cheeks inflated with exasperation.

"Why, that's the guy, Chief, that threatened to get you."

"I'm quite aware of that fact," said Markham coldly; then he added in a somewhat softened tone: "Sit down, Sergeant. Consider yourself off duty for the moment, and have a drink of your favorite whisky."

When Heath had adjusted himself in a chair, Markham went on.

"Surely you don't expect me, at this late date, to begin taking seriously the hysterical mouthings of criminals I have convicted in the course of my duties."

"But, Chief, this guy's a tough *hombre,* and he ain't the forgetting or the forgiving kind."

"Anyway,"—Markham laughed without concern—"it would be tomorrow, at the earliest, before he could reach New York."

As Heath and Markham were speaking, Vance's eyebrows rose in mild curiosity.

"I say, Markham, all I've been able to glean is that your tutel'ry Sergeant has fears for your curtailed existence, and that you yourself are rather annoyed by his zealous worries."

"Hell, Mr. Vance, I'm not worryin'," Heath blurted. "I'm just considering the possibilities, as you might say."

"Yes, yes, I know," smiled Vance. "Always careful. Sewin' up seams that haven't even ripped. Doughty and admirable, as always, Sergeant. But whence springeth your qualm?"

"I'm sorry, Vance." Markham apologized for his failure to explain. "It's really of no importance—just a routine telegraphic announcement of a rather commonplace jail-break at Nomenica.* Three men under long sentences staged the exodus, and two of them were shot by the guards..."

"I'm not botherin' about the guys who was shot," Heath cut in. "It's the other one—the guy that got away safe—that's set me to thinkin'—"

"And who might this stimulator of thought be, Sergeant?" Vance asked.

"Benny the Buzzard!" whispered Heath, with melodramatic emphasis.

"Ah!" Vance smiled. "An ornithological specimen—*Buteo borealis*. Maybe he flew away to freedom..."

"It's no laughing matter, Mr. Vance." Heath became even more serious. "Benny the Buzzard—or Benny Pellinzi, to give him his honest monicker—is plenty tough, in spite of looking like a bloodless, pretty-faced boy. Only a few years back, he was strutting around telling anybody who'd listen that he was Public Enemy Number One. That type of guy. But he was only small change, except for his toughness and meanness—actually nothing but a dumb, stupid rat—"

"Rat? Buzzard?... My word, Sergeant, aren't you confusin' your natural history?"

"And only three years ago," continued Heath doggedly, "Mr. Markham got him sent up for a twenty-year stretch. And he pulls a jail-break just this afternoon and gets away with it. Sweet, ain't it?"

"Still," submitted Vance, "such A.W.O.L.s have been taken ere this."

"Sure they have." Heath extended his off-duty respite and took another whisky. "But you must've read what this guy pulled in court when he was sentenced. The judge hadn't hardly

---

*   *Nomenica, southwest of Buffalo, was the westernmost State prison in New York.*

finished slipping him the twenty years when he blew off his gauge. He pointed at Mr. Markham and, at the top of his voice, swore some kind of cockeyed oath that he'd come back and get him if it was the last thing he ever did. And he sounded like he meant it. He was so sore and steamed up that it took two man-eating bailiffs to drag him out of the courtroom. Generally it's the judge who gets the threats; but this guy elected to take it out on the D. A. And that somehow made more sense."

Vance nodded slowly.

"Yes, quite—quite. I see your point, Sergeant. Different and therefore dangerous."

"And why I really came here tonight," Heath went on, "was to tell Mr. Markham what I intended doing. Naturally, we'll be on the lookout for the Buzzard. He might come here direct, all right; and he might head west and try to reach the Dakotas—the Bad Lands for him, if he's got a brain."

"Exactly," Markham interpolated. "You're probably right when you suggest he'll head west. And I'm certainly planning no immediate jaunt to the Black Hills."

"Anyhow, Chief," the Sergeant persisted stubbornly, "I'm not taking any chances on him—especially since we've got a pretty good line on his old cronies in this burg."

"Just what line do you refer to, Sergeant?"

"Mirche, and the *Domdaniel* café, and Benny's old sweetie that sings there—the Del Marr jane."

"Whether Mirche and Pellinzi are cronies," said Markham, "is a moot question in my mind."

"It ain't in mine, Chief. And if the Buzzard *should* sneak back to New York, I've got a hunch he'd go straight to Mirche for help."

Markham did not argue the possibilities further. Instead, he merely asked: "What course do you intend to pursue, Sergeant?"

Heath leaned across the table.

"I figure it this way, Chief. If the Buzzard *does* plan to return to his old hunting grounds, he'll be smart about it. He'll do it quick and sudden-like, figurin' we haven't got set. If he don't show up in the next few days I'll simply drop the idea, and the boys'll keep their eyes open in the routine way. But— beginning tomorrow morning, I plan to have Hennessey in that old rooming-house across from the *Domdaniel*, covering the little door leading into Mirche's private office. An' Burke and Snitkin will be with Hennessey in case the bird does show up."

"Aren't you a bit optimistic, Sergeant?" asked Vance. "Three years in prison can work many changes in a man's appearance, especially if the victim is still young and not too robust."

Heath dismissed Vance's skepticism with an impatient gesture.

"I'll trust Hennessey—he's got a good eye."

"Oh, I'm not questioning Hennessey's vision," Vance assured him, "—provided your liberty-lovin' Buzzard should be so foolish as to choose the front door for his entry into Mirche's office. But really, my dear Sergeant, Maestro Pellinzi may deem it wiser to steal in by the rear door, don't y' know."

"There ain't no rear door," explained Heath. "And there ain't no side door, either. A strictly private room with only one entrance facing the street. That's the wide-open and aboveboard set-up of this guy Mirche—everything on the up-and-up. Slick as they come."

"Is this sanctum a separate structure?" asked Vance. "Or is it an annex to the café? I don't seem to recall it."

"No. And you wouldn't notice it, if you weren't looking for it. It's like an end room that's been cut off in the corner of the building—the way they cut off a doctor's office, or a small shop, in a big apartment-house. But if you wanta see Mirche that's where you'll most likely find him. The place looks as innocent as an old ladies' home."

Heath glanced round at us significantly as he continued.

"And yet, plenty goes on in that little room. If I could ever get a dictograph planted there, the D. A.'s office would have enough underworld trials on its hands to keep it busy from now on."

He paused and cocked an eye at Markham.

"How do you feel about my idea for tomorrow?"

"It can't do any harm, Sergeant," answered Markham without enthusiasm. "But I still think it would be a waste of time and energy."

"Maybe so." Heath finished his whisky. "But I feel I gotta follow my hunch, just the same."

Vance set down his liqueur glass, and a whimsical expression came into his eyes.

"But I say, Markham," he drawled, "it would be a waste of time and energy, no matter what the outcome. Ah, your precious law, and its prissy procedure! How you Solons complicate the simple things of life! Even if this red-tailed hawk with the operatic name should appear among his olden haunts and be snared in the Sergeant's seine, you would still treat him kindly and caressingly under the euphemistic phrase, 'due process of law.' You'd coddle him no end. You'd take all possible precautions to bring him in alive, although he himself might blow the brains out of a couple of the Sergeant's confrères. Then you'd lodge and nourish him well; you'd drive him through town in a high-powered limousine; you'd give him a pleasant scenic trip back to Nomenica. And all for what, old dear? For the highly questionable privilege of supportin' him elegantly for life."

Markham was obviously nettled.

"I suppose *you* could settle the whole situation with a lirp."

"It could be, don't y' know." Vance was in one of his tantalizing moods. "Here's a worthless johnnie who has long been a thorn in the side of the law; who has, as you jolly well know, killed a man and been convicted accordingly; who has engineered a lawless prison break costing two more lives; who has promised to murder you in cold blood; and who is even now deprivin' the Sergeant of his slumber. Not a nice person, Markham. And all these irregularities might be so easily and expeditiously adjusted by shooting the johnnie on sight, or otherwise disposing of him quickly, without ado or *chinoiserie*."

"And I suppose"—Markham spoke almost angrily—"that you yourself would be willing to undertake this illegal purge."

"Willing?" There was a teasing tone in Vance's voice. "I'd be positively delighted. My good deed for that day."

Markham puffed vigorously at his cigar. He was always irritated when Vance's persiflage took this line.

"Deliberately taking a human life, Vance—"

"Please spare me the logion, Reverend Doctor. I know the answer. With Society and Law and Order singing the Greek chorus *a capella*. But you must admit my suggested solution is logical, practical, and just."

"We've gone into that sophistry before," snapped Markham. "And furthermore, I'm not going to let you spoil my dinner with such nonsensical chatter."

CHAPTER TWO

A Rustic Interlude
(Saturday, May 18; afternoon.)

THE NEXT DAY, shortly after noon, we met Markham in his dingy private office overlooking the Tombs. Ordinarily the District Attorney's office was closed at this hour on Saturdays, but Markham was in the meshes of a trying political tangle and wished to see the affair settled as soon as possible.

"I'm deuced sorry, don't y' know," said Vance, "that you must slave on an afternoon like this. I was hoping you might be persuaded to come for a drive over the countryside."

"What!" exclaimed Markham in mock surprise. "Are you succumbing to your natural impulses? Don't tell me Mother Nature's sirenical tones can sway a hothouse sybarite like yourself! Why not have Van lash you to the mast in true Odyssean manner?"

"No. I find myself actually longin' for the spell of an Ogygian isle with citron scent and cedar-sawn—"

"And perhaps a wood-nymph like Calypso."

"My dear Markham! Really, now!" Vance pretended indignation. "No—oh, no. I merely plan a bit of gambolin' in the Bronx greenery."

"I see that the clear-toned Sirens of the flowered fields have snared you." Markham's smile was playfully derisive. "If Heath's ominous dream is fulfilled we'll later be steering a stormy course between Scylla and Charybdis."

"One never knows, does one? But should it come to pass, I trust no man shall be caught from out our hollow ship by the voracious Scylla."

"For Heaven's sake, Vance, don't be so gloomy. You're talking utter nonsense."

(I particularly remember this bit of classical repartee which certainly would not have found its way into this record, had it not been that it proved curiously prophetic, even to the scent of citron and the Messina monster's cave.)

"And I suppose," suggested Markham, "you'll do your gamboling in immaculate attire. I somehow can't picture you in vagabondian trappings."

"You're quite wrong," said Vance. "I shall don a rugged old tweed suit—the most ancient bit of coverin' I possess... But tell me, Markham, how goes it with the zealous Sergeant and his premonitions?"

"Oh, I suppose he's gone ahead with his useless arrangements." Markham spoke with indifference. "But if poor Hennessey has to invite strabismus for very long I'll have more to fear from *him* in the way of retribution than from Mr. Beniamino Pellinzi... I don't quite understand Heath's sudden case of jitters over my safety."

"Stout fella, Heath." Vance studied the ash on his cigarette with a hesitant smile. "Fact is, Markham, I intend to partake of Mirche's expensive hospitality tonight myself."

"You too!... You're actually going to the *Domdaniel* tonight?"

"Not in the hope of encounterin' your friend the Buzzard,"
replied Vance. "But Heath has stirred my curiosity. I should
like to take a closer look at the incredible Mr. Mirche. I've seen
him before, of course, at his hospice, but I've never really paid
attention to his features. And I could bear a peep—from the
outside only, of course—at this mysterious office which has so
fretted the Sergeant's imagination... And there's always the
chance a little excitement may ensue when the early portentous
shadows of the mysterious night—"

"Come, come, Vance. You sound like a penny dreadful.
What *arrière pensée* is being screened by this smoke of words?"

"If you really must know, Markham, the food is excellent at the *Domdaniel*. I was merely tryin' to hide a *gourmet*'s
yearnin'..."

Markham snorted, and the talk shifted to a discussion of
other matters, interrupted now and then by telephone calls.
When Markham had completed his arrangements for the
afternoon and evening, he ushered us out through the judges'
private chambers and down to the street.

After a brief lunch we drove Markham back to his office, and
then headed uptown to Vance's apartment. Here Vance changed
his suit for the old disreputable tweed, and put on heavier boots
and a soft well-worn Homburg hat. Then we went out again to his
Hispano-Suiza, and in an hour's time we were driving leisurely
along Palisade Avenue in the Riverdale section of the Bronx.

Both sides of the road were thickly grown with trees and
shrubs. The fragrance of spring flowers hung in the air, and we
caught a fleck of bright color now and then. On our left, beyond
an unbroken steel-mesh fence, a gentle slope dipped to the
Hudson. On the right the ground rose more abruptly, so that
the rough stone wall did not shut off the prospect.

At the top of a slight incline, just where the road swung
inland, Vance turned off the roadway, and brought the car to
a gentle stop.

"This, I think, would be an ideal spot for minglin' with the
flora and communin' with nature."

Except for the fence on the river side, and the stone wall, perhaps five feet high, along the inner border of the road, we were, to all appearances, on a lonely country road. Vance crossed the broad and shaded grassy strip that stretched like a runner of green carpet between the roadway and the wall. He clambered up the stone enclosure, beckoning me to do likewise as he disappeared in the lush rustic foliage on the farther side.

For over an hour we trudged back and forth through the woods, and then, as we suddenly came face to face with the stone enclosure again, Vance reluctantly looked at his watch.

"Almost five," he said. "We'd better be staggerin' home, Van."

I preceded him to the roadway, and started slowly back toward the car. A large automobile, running almost noise-lessly, suddenly came round the turn. I stopped as it sped by, and watched it disappear over the edge of the hill. Then I continued in the direction of our own car.

After a few steps, I became aware of a young woman standing near the wall, well back from the roadway, in a secluded grassy bower. She was shaking the front of her skirt nervously and with marked agitation, and was stamping one foot in the soft loam. She looked perturbed and displeased, and as I drew nearer I saw that on the front of her flimsy summer frock there was an inch-wide burnt hole.

As a vexed exclamation escaped her, Vance leaped—or, I should say, fell—from the wall behind her. His heel caught in the crude masonry, and as he strove to regain his balance, a sharp projection of the plaster tore the sleeve of his coat. The unexpected commotion startled the young woman anew, and she turned, inquisitively alert.

She was a petite creature, and gracefully animated, with a piquant oval face and regular, sensitive features. Her eyes were large and brown, with extremely long lashes curling over them. A straight and slender nose lent dignity and character to a mouth made for smiling. She was slim and supple, and seemed to fit in perfectly with her pastoral surroundings.

"My word!" murmured Vance, looking down at her. "That wasn't a very graceful entry into your arbor. Please forgive me if I frightened you."

The girl continued to stare at him distrustfully, and as I looked at Vance again I could well understand her reaction. He was quite disheveled; his shoes and trousers were generously spattered with mud; his hat was crushed and grotesquely awry; and his torn coat-sleeve looked like that of some roving mendicant.

In a moment the girl smiled.

"Oh, I'm not frightened," she assured him in a musical voice which had a very youthful engaging timbre. "I'm just angry. Terribly angry. Were you ever angry?... But I'm not angry with *you*, for I don't even know you... Maybe I would be angry with you if I knew you... Did you ever think of that?"

"Yes—yes. Quite often." Vance laughed and removed his hat: immediately he looked far more presentable. "And I'm sure you'd be entirely justified, too... By the by, may I sit down? I'm beastly tired, don't y' know."

The girl looked quickly up the road, and then seated herself rather abruptly, much as a child might throw herself carelessly on the ground.

"That would be wonderful. I'll read your palm. Have you ever had your palm read? I'm very good at it. Delpha taught me all the lines. Delpha knows all about the hands, and the stars, and lucky numbers. She's a fortune-teller. And she's psychic, too. Just like me. I'm psychic. Are you psychic? But maybe I can't concentrate today." Her voice took on a mystic quality. "Some days, when I'm feeling in tune, I could tell you how old you are and how many children you have..."

Vance laughed, and seated himself beside her.

"But really, y' know, I don't think I could bear to learn such staggerin' facts about myself just now..."

Vance took out his cigarette case and opened it slowly.

"I'm sure you wouldn't mind if I smoked," he said ingratiatingly, holding out the case to her; but receiving only a giggle and a shake of the head, he lighted one of his *Régies* for himself.

"But I'm awfully glad you mentioned cigarettes," the girl said. "It reminds me how mad I was."

"Oh, yes." Vance smiled indulgently. "But won't you tell me at whom you were so angry?"

She squinted at the cigarette between his fingers.

"I don't know now," she answered with slight confusion.

"By Jove, that's unfortunate. Maybe it was me you were angry at all the time?"

"No, it wasn't you—at least, I didn't think it was you. Now I'm not so sure. At first I thought it was somebody in a big car that just went by—"

"And *what* were you angry about?"

"Oh, that... Well, look at the front of my new dress here." She spread the skirt about her. "Do you see that big burnt hole? It's just ruined. And I simply adore this dress. Don't you like it?—that is, if it wasn't burnt? I made it myself—well, anyhow, I told mother how I wanted it made. It made me look *awfully* cute. And now I can't wear it any more." There was real distress in her tone. "Did *you* throw that lighted cigarette?"

"What cigarette?" asked Vance.

"Why, the cigarette that burnt my dress. It's around here somewhere... Well, anyhow, it was an awfully good shot, especially since you couldn't see me. And maybe you didn't even know I was here. And that would make it much harder to hit me, don't you think?"

"Yes, I can see your point." Vance was as much interested as he was amused. "But really, my dear, it must have been some villain in the car—if there was a car."

The girl sighed.

"Well, then," she murmured with resignation, "I guess it wasn't you I was mad at. And now I don't know who it was. And that makes me madder than ever. I'm sure if I was mad at *you*, you'd do something about it."

"Shall we say then, that I'm just as sorry about it as if I had thrown the cigarette?" suggested Vance.

"But *now* I don't know whether you did or not. If you couldn't see me through the wall, how could I see you?"

"Irrefragable logic!" Vance returned, adjusting himself to her seemingly fanciful mood. "Therefore, you must permit me to make amends—no matter who the culprit was."

"Really," she said, "I don't know what you mean." But a twinkle in her eyes seemed to belie the words.

"I mean just this: I want you to go down to Chareau and Lyons* and select one of their prettiest frocks—one which will make you look just as cute as this one does."

"Oh, I couldn't afford it!"

He took out his card case, and, jotting a few words on one of his visiting cards, tucked it beneath the flap of the girl's handbag which was lying on the grass.

"You just take that card to Mr. Lyons himself and tell him I sent you."

Her eyes beamed gratefully, and she did not protest further.

"As you quite correctly say," Vance continued, "you couldn't see through the wall, and I therefore see no human way of proving that I did *not* throw the cigarette."

"Well, now, that's settled, isn't it?" The girl giggled again. "I'm so glad it was *you* I was mad at for throwing the cigarette."

"And so am I," asserted Vance. "And, incidentally, I also hope you'll use the same perfume when you wear your new dress. It's somehow just like the springtime—a 'delicious scent of citron and orange trees,' as Longfellow pæaned in his *Wayside Inn*."

"Oh, did he?"

"By the by, what is it? I don't recognize it as any of the popular scents."

"I don't know," the girl replied. "I guess nobody knows. It hasn't any name. Imagine not having a name! If we didn't

---

*   *Chareau and Lyons was at that time one of the more exclusive and fashionable dress shops of New York.*

have names we'd get terribly mixed up, wouldn't we?... It was made specially for me by George—but I suppose I shouldn't really call him George to strangers. His name is Mr. Burns. I'm his assistant at the In-O-Scent Corporation—that's a big perfume factory. He's always mixing different things together and smelling them. That's his job. He's very clever too. Only, he's *much* too serious. But I don't think he mixed any citron in it—I really don't know exactly what citron smells like. I thought it was something you put in cake."

"It's the preserved rind of the citron that goes into cake," Vance explained. "The oil of citron is quite different. It has the odor of citronella and lemons; and when it is treated with sulphuric acid it even has the odor of violets."

"Isn't that *wonderful!*" she exclaimed. "Why, you sound *just* like George. He's always saying things like that. I'm sure Mr. Burns knows all about it. He gets me so mixed up sometimes, bringing him the right bottles of extracts and essences. And he's *so* particular about it. Sometimes he even says I don't know how to boil his old flasks and tubes and graduates. Imagine!"

"But I'm sure," Vance asserted, "that you brought him the right phials when he prepared the odor you are wearing. And I'm sure one of them contained citron, though it may have had some other name... And speaking of names, is *your* name, by any chance, Calypso?"

She shook her head.

"No, but it's something almost like that. It's Gracie Allen."

Vance smiled, and the girl's chatter took still another direction.

"But aren't you going to tell me what you were doing over beyond the wall? You know, that's private property, and I wouldn't go in there for anything. It wouldn't be right. Would it? And anyhow, I don't know where there's a gate. But this is nice out here. I've come here several times, and yet no one's ever thrown lighted cigarettes at me before, although I've been right in this same spot many times. But I guess everything has to happen the first time sometime. Have you ever thought of that?"

"Yes—oh, yes. It's a profound question." He chuckled. "But aren't you afraid to come to such an unfrequented spot alone?"

"Alone?" Again the girl glanced up the road. "I don't come alone. I generally come with a friend who lives over toward Broadway. His name is Mr. Puttle, and he works in the same business house I do. Mr. Puttle's a salesman. And Mr. Burns—I told you about him before—was very angry with me for coming out here this afternoon with Mr. Puttle. But he's *always* angry when I go anywhere with anybody else, and *especially* if it's Mr. Puttle. Don't you think that's silly?" She made a self-satisfied moue.

"And where might Mr. Puttle be now?" asked Vance. "Don't tell me he's attempting to sell perfumes along the highways and byways of Riverdale."

"Oh, goodness, no! He *never* works on Saturday afternoons. And neither do I. I really think the brain should have a rest now and then, don't you?... Oh, you asked me where Mr. Puttle is. Well, I'll tell you—I'm sure he wouldn't mind. He's gone to look for a nunnery."

"A nunnery? Good Heavens! What for?"

"He said there was a lovely view from there, with benches and flowers and everything. But he didn't know whether it was up the road from here or down. So I told him to find out first. I didn't feel like going to a nunnery when I didn't even know where it was. Would you go to a nunnery if you didn't know where it was—especially if your shoes hurt you?"

"No, I think you were eminently sensible. But *I* happen to know where it is; it's quite a distance down the other way."

"Well, Jimmy—that is, Mr. Puttle—has gone in the wrong direction then. That's just like him. I'm lucky I made him look first..."

CHAPTER THREE

The Startling Adventure
(Saturday, May 18; 5:30 p.m.)

THE GIRL LEANED forward, and looked at Vance with impulsive eagerness.

"But I forgot: I'm just dying to know what you were doing on the other side of the wall. I do hope it was exciting. I'm *very* romantic, you know. Are you romantic? I mean, I just *love* excitement and thrills. And it's so thrilling and exciting along here—especially with that high wall. I know you must have been having a simply *wonderful* adventure of some kind. All kinds of thrilling and exciting things happen inside of walls. People don't just build walls for nothing, do they?"

"No—rarely." Vance shook his head in pretended earnestness. "People generally have a very good reason for building walls, such as: to keep other people out—or, sometimes, to keep them in."

"You see, I was right!... And now tell me," she pleaded, "what wild, exciting adventure did you have there?"

Vance drew a deep puff on his cigarette.

"Really, y' know," he said with a mock seriousness, "I'm afraid to breathe a word of it to anyone... By the by, just how exciting do you like your adventures?"

"Oh, they must be *terribly* exciting—and dangerous—and dark—and filled with the spirit of revenge. You know, like a *murder*—maybe a murder for love..."

"That's it!" Vance slapped his knee. "Now I can tell you everything—I know you'll understand." He lowered his voice to an intimate, sepulchral whisper. "When I came dashing so ungracefully over the wall, I had just committed a murder."

"How simply wonderful!" But I noticed she edged away from him a bit.

"That's why I was running away so fast," Vance went on.

"I think you're joking." The girl was at her ease again. "But go on."

"It was really an act of altruism," Vance continued, seeming to take genuine enjoyment in his fantastic tale. "I did it for a friend—to save a friend from danger—from *revenge*."

"He must have been a very bad man. I'm sure he deserved to die and that you did a noble deed—like the heroes of olden times. *They* didn't wait for the police and the law and all those things. They just rode forth and fixed everything up—just like that." She snapped her fingers, and I could not help thinking of Markham's sarcastic allusion to Vance's conclusive "lirp" the previous evening.

Vance studied her in sombre astonishment.

" 'Out of the mouth of babes—' " he began.

"What?" Her brow furrowed.

"Nothing, really." And Vance laughed under his breath... "Well, to continue with my dark confession: I knew this man was a very dangerous person, and that my friend's life was in peril. So I came out here this afternoon, and back there, in yon shady wood, where no one could see, I killed him... I am so glad you think I did right."

His fabricated story, based on his conversation with Markham the night before, fitted in well with the girl's unexpected request for an exciting adventure.

"And what was the murdered man's name?" she asked. "I hope it was a terrible name. I always say people have *just* the names they deserve. It's like numerology—only it's different. If you have a certain number of letters in your name, it isn't like having a different number of letters, is it? It means something, too. Delpha told me."

"What names do you especially like?" Vance asked.

"Well, let me see. Burns is a pretty name, don't you think?"

"Yes, I do." Vance smiled pleasantly. "Incidentally, it's Scotch—"

"But George isn't a *bit* Scotch," the girl protested indignantly. "He's *awfully* generous."

"No, no," Vance hastened to assure her. "Not Scotch like that. I was going to say that it's Scotch for 'brook' or 'rivulet'...."

"Oh, water! That's different. You see, I was right!" she chirped; then nodded sagely. "Water! That's George! He *never* drinks—you know, liquor. He says it affects his nose, so he can't smell."

"Smell?"

"Uh-huh. George has simply *got* to smell—it's his job. Smelling odors, and knowing which one will sell big, and which one will make you a vamp, and which one is bad enough for hotel soap. He's *terribly* clever that way. He even invented *In-O-Scent*—mixed it all himself. And Mr. Doolson—he's our boss—named the new factory for George. Well, not exactly for George, but you know what I mean."

Pride shone in her eyes.

"And oh!" she ran on; "George has five letters in his name—honest—just you count them—B-U-R-N-S. And I've got five letters in *my* last name, too. Isn't that funny? But it means something—something *important*. It's—it's science. I vibrate to five. But six is *awfully* unlucky for me. I'm allergic— that's what Delpha calls it—to six. It's very scientific—*really*!"

"Mr. Puttle has six letters in his name," said Vance, with a puckish glance at her.

"That's right. I've thought of that... Oh, well... But I forgot—what was the name of the man you so bravely killed?"

"He had a very unpleasant name. He was called Benny the Buzzard."

The girl's head bobbed up and down vigorously in complete understanding.

"Yes, that's a *very* bad name. It's got—let me see—*seven* letters. Oh! That's a mystical number. It's sort of like Fate!"

"Well, he was sent to prison for twenty years." Vance resumed his ingenious recital. "But he broke away and escaped only yesterday, and came back to New York to kill my friend."

"Oh, then there will be headlines in all the papers tomorrow about your murdering him!"

"My word! I hope not." Vance pretended a show of great concern. "I feel I have done a good deed, but I do hope, don't y' know, I am not found out. And I am sure *you* wouldn't tell anyone, would you?"

"Oh, no," the girl assured him.

Vance heaved an exaggerated sigh, and slowly rose to his feet.

"Well, I must get into hiding," he said, "before the police learn of my crime. Another hour or so and—who knows?—they may be after me."

"Oh, policemen are so silly." She pouted. "They're always getting people into trouble. Do you know?—if everybody was good we wouldn't need any policemen, would we?"

"No-o—"

"And if we didn't have any policemen, we wouldn't need to bother about being good, would we?"

"My word!" Vance murmured. "Do you, by any chance, happen to be a philosopher in disguise?"

She seemed astonished. "Why, *this* isn't a disguise. I only wore a disguise once—when I was a little girl. I went to a party disguised as a fairy."

Vance smiled admiringly.

"I'm sure," he said, "it was quite a needless costume. You'll never need a disguise, my dear, to pass as a most charming fairy... Would you care to shake hands with a dyed-in-the-wool villain?"

She put her hand in his.

"You're not *really* a villain. Why, you only murdered one bad man. And thank you so much for the lovely new dress," she added. "Did you really mean it?"

"I really did." His sincerity dissipated any remaining doubt. "And good luck with Mr. Puttle—and Mr. Burns."

She waved solemnly as we made our way down the dusty road toward our car. Vance was occupied with lighting another *Régie*, and as we turned the bend of the road I looked back. A dapper young man stood before the girl; and I knew that Mr. Puttle, the perfumery salesman, had returned from his fruitless quest for the nunnery.

"What an amazin' creature!" murmured Vance, as we climbed into the car and drove off. "I really think she half believes my dramatization of the Sergeant's fears and my ribbing of Markham. There's naïveté, Van. Or, mayhap, a basically shrewd nature, plethoric with romance, striving to live among the clouds in this sordid world. And living by the manufacture of perfume. What an incredible combination of circumstances! And all mixed up with springtime—and visions of heroics—and young love."

I looked at him questioningly.

"Quite," he repeated. "That was definitely indicated. But I fear that Mr. Puttle's long jaunts from upper Broadway will come to naught in the end. You noted that she anointed herself with the fragrant aroma of Mr. Burns' nameless concoction, even when transiently countrysiding with Mr. Puttle. All signs considered, I regard the mixer and smeller of the subtle scents of Araby as the odds-on favorite to win the Lovin' Cup."

CHAPTER FOUR

The Domdaniel Café
(Saturday, May 18; 8 p.m.)

THE *DOMDANIEL CAFÉ*, situated in West 50th Street
near Seventh Avenue, had for many years attracted a general
and varied clientele. The remodeling of the large old mansion
in which the café was housed had been tastefully achieved, and
much of the old air of solidity and durability remained.

From either side of the wide entrance to the ends of
the building ran a narrow open terrace attractively studded
with pseudo-Grecian pots of neatly trimmed privet. At the
western end of the house a delivery alley separated the café
from the neighboring edifice. At the east side there was a
paved driveway, perhaps ten feet wide, passing under an ivy-
draped *porte-cochère* to the garage in the rear. A commercial
skyscraper at the corner of Seventh Avenue abutted on this
driveway.

It was nearly eight o'clock when we arrived that mild May evening. Lighting a cigarette, Vance peered into the shadows of the *porte-cochère* and the dimly lighted area beyond. He then sauntered for a short distance into this narrow approach, and gazed at the ivy-covered windows and side door almost hidden from the street. In a few moments he rejoined me on the sidewalk and turned his seemingly casual attention to the front of the building.

"Ah!" he murmured. "There's the entrance to Señor Mirche's mysterious office which so strangely inflamed the Sergeant's hormones. Probably a window enlarged, when the old house was remodeled. Merely utilitarian, don't y' know."

It was, as Vance observed, an unpretentious door opening directly on the narrow terrace; and two sturdy wooden steps led down to the sidewalk. At each side of the door was a small window—or, I should say, an opening like a machicolation—securely barred with a wrought-iron grille.

"The office has a larger window at the side, overlooking the tessellated driveway," said Vance; "and that, too, is closely grilled. The light from without must be rather inadequate when, as the Sergeant seems to think, Mr. Mirche is engaged in his nefarious plottin's."

To my surprise, Vance went up the wooden steps to the terrace and casually peered through one of the narrow windows into the office.

"The office appears to be quite as honest and upright inside as it does from out here," he said. "I fear the suspicious Sergeant is a victim of nightmares…"

He turned and looked across the street at the rooming-house. Two adjoining windows on the second floor, directly opposite the small corner door of the *Domdaniel*, were dark.

"Poor Hennessey!" sighed Vance. "Behind one of those sombre squares of blackness he is watchin' and hopin'. Symbolic of all mankind… Ah, well, let's not tarry longer. I have amorous visions of a *fricandeau de veau Macédoine*. I trust the chef has lost none of his cunning since last I was here. Then, it was really sublime."

We walked on to the main entrance, and were greeted in the impressive reception hall by the unctuous Mr. Mirche himself. He seemed well pleased to see Vance, whom he addressed by name, and turned us over to the head waiter, pompously exhorting our *cicerone* that we be given every attention and consideration.

The rejuvenated interior of the *Domdaniel* had a far more modern appearance than did the exterior. Withal, much of the charm of another day still lingered in the panels of carved wood and the scrolled banisters of the stairway, and in a wide fireplace which had been left intact at one side of the huge main room.

We could not have selected a better table than the one to which we were led. It was near the fireplace, and since the tables along the walls were slightly elevated, we had an unobstructed view of the entire room. Far on our right was the main entrance, and on our left the orchestra stand. Opposite us, at the other end of the room, an archway led to the hall; and beyond that, almost as if framed in the doorway, we could see the wide carpeted stairs to the floor above.

Vance glanced over the room cursorily and then gave his attention to ordering the dinner. This accomplished, he leaned back in his chair and, lighting a *Régie*, relaxed comfortably. But I noted that, from under his half-closed eyelids, he was scrutinizing the people about us. Suddenly he straightened up in his chair, and leaning toward me, murmured:

"My word! My aging eyes must be playing tricks on me. I say, peep far over on my right, near the entrance. It's the astonishing young woman of the citron scent. And she's having a jolly time. She is accompanied by a youthful swain in sartorial splendor... I wonder whether it is her explorin' escort in Riverdale, or the more serious teetotaler, Mr. Burns. Whoever it is, he is being most attentive, and is pleased with himself no end."

At once I recognized the elegant young man of whom I had caught a glimpse as we rounded the turn on Palisade

Avenue on our way back to the car. I informed Vance that it was undoubtedly Mr. Puttle.

"I'm in no way surprised," was his response. "The young woman is obviously following the approved and time-honored technique. Puttle will receive, alas! an overwhelming percentage of her favors until the really important moment of final decision is at hand. Then, I opine, the beneficiary will be the neglected Burns." He laughed softly. "The chicaneries of *amour* never change. If only Burns himself were on the scene tonight, separate and apart, glowerin' with jealousy, and eatin' out his heart!" He smiled with wistful amusement.

His glance roved about the room again as he puffed lazily on his cigarette. Before long his eyes rested quizzically on a man alone at a small table near the far corner.

"Really, y' know, I believe I have found our Mr. Burns, the dolorous hypotenuse of my imagin'ry triangle. At least the gentleman fulfills all the requirements. He is alone. He is of a suitable age. He is serious. He sits at a table placed at just the right angle to observe his strayin' wood-nymph and her companion. He is watching her rather closely and seems displeased and jealous enough to be contemplating murder. He has no appetite for the food before him. He has no wine or other alcoholic beverage. *And*—he is actually glowerin'!"

I let my gaze follow Vance's as he spoke, and I observed the lonely young man. His face was stern and somewhat rugged. Despite the sense of humor denoted by the upward angle of his eyebrows, his broad forehead gave the impression of considerable depth of thought and a capacity for accurate judgment. His gray eyes were set well apart, and engaging in their candor; and his chin was firm, yet sensitive. He was dressed neatly and unostentatiously, in severe contrast with the showy grandeur of Mr. Puttle.

During an intermission in the floor show the lone young man in question rose rather hesitantly from his chair and walked with determined strides to the table occupied by Miss Allen and her companion. They greeted him without enthusiasm. The newcomer, frowning unpleasantly, made no attempt to be cordial.

The young woman raised her eyebrows with a histrionic *hauteur* altogether incongruous with the elfish cast of her features. Her companion's manner was *dégagé* and palpably condescending—his was the rôle of the victor over a conquered and harassed enemy. His effect upon Burns—if it *was* Burns—must have been exceedingly gratifying to him. Combined with the young woman's simulated disdain, it perceptibly enhanced the interloper's gloom. He made an awkward gesture of defeat, and, turning away, went despondently back to his table. However, I noticed that Miss Allen shot several covert glances in his direction—which suggested that she was far from being the indifferent damsel she had pretended to be.

Vance had watched the little drama with delighted interest.

"And now, Van," he said, "the canvas of young love is quite complete. Ah, the eternally sadistic, yet loyal, heart of woman!…"

Fifteen or twenty minutes later Mirche, beaming and bowing, came into the dining room from the main entrance hall, and passed on toward the rear of the room to a small table just behind the orchestra dais, at which one of the entertainers sat. She was a blonde and flashingly handsome woman whom I knew to be the well-known singer Dixie Del Marr.

She greeted Mirche with a smile which seemed more intimate than would be expected from an employee to an employer. Mirche drew out the chair facing her and sat down. I was somewhat surprised to note that Vance was watching them closely, and felt that this was no idle curiosity on his part.

I turned my gaze again to the singer's table. Dixie Del Marr and Mirche had begun what appeared to be a confidential chat. They were leaning toward each other, evidently wishing to avoid being overheard by those about them. Mirche was emphasizing some point, and Dixie Del Marr was nodding in agreement. Then Miss Del Marr made some answering remark to which he, in turn, nodded understandingly.

After a brief continuation of their conversation in this overt, yet secretive, manner, they both sat back in their chairs, and Mirche gave an order to a passing waiter. A few moments later the waiter returned with two slender glasses of rose-colored liquid.

"Very interestin'," murmured Vance. "I wonder..."

CHAPTER FIVE

A Rendezvous
(Saturday, May 18; 9:30 p.m.)

IT WAS SHORTLY thereafter that I noticed Gracie Allen rise gayly from her seat beside the self-satisfied Mr. Puttle. She waved to him coyly as she sallied forth across the dining room, like a graceful gazelle.

"My word!" chuckled Vance. "The astonishin' wood-nymph is coming our way. If she recognizes me, my tall tale of derring-do this afternoon will crumble to dust about my mendacious head..."

Even as he spoke, she spied him, threw up her hands in rapturous surprise, and came to our table.

"Why, hello," she sang out; and then reprimanded Vance in lower tones: "You're a terribly bold murderer. Oh, *awfully* bold. Don't you know that someone is apt to see you here? You know, like a waiter, or somebody."

"Or you, yourself," smiled Vance.

"Oh, but *I* wouldn't tell. Don't you remember? I *promised* not to tell." She sat down with startling suddenness, and giggled musically. "And I always say everybody should keep a promise, if you know what I mean... But my brother's funny that way. He doesn't *ever* keep a promise. But he keeps lots of other things. And sometimes he gets into awful trouble by not keeping a promise. He's always getting into trouble. Maybe it's because he's so ambitious. Are you ambitious?"

"Speaking of promises," said Vance, "do you keep all your promises to Mr. Burns?"

"I *never* made any promise to George," she assured Vance, the tinge of a confused blush mounting her saucy features. "Whatever made you think of that? But he's tried awfully hard to make me promise him something. And he gets *terribly* angry with me. He's angry tonight. But, of course, he wouldn't show it in front of so many people. He's so *very* dignified. No one can ever tell what he's thinking about. But nobody can tell what *I'm* thinking about, either. Only, I'm not dignified. Mr. Puttle says I'm just cute and attractive. And he's known me a long time. And I think it's much better to be cute and attractive than to be dignified. Don't you?"

Vance made no effort to restrain his mirth.

"I certainly do think so," he answered. "And by the by, where is the dignified Mr. Burns this evening?"

The girl tittered with embarrassment.

"He's sitting over there across the room." She turned her head gracefully, to indicate the lone young man who had previously attracted our attention. "And he seems very unhappy, too. I can't *imagine* why he came here tonight—I know he's never been here before... Do you want to know a secret? Well, I'll tell you, anyhow. *I* was never here before, either. But I really like it here. Don't you? It's awfully big—and noisy. And there's so many people. Don't you like a lot of people in one place? I think that people are *terribly* nice. But I'm afraid George doesn't like it here. Maybe that's why he's so unhappy."

Vance did not interrupt her. He seemed to find pleasant diversion in her inconsequential rambling.

"And oh!" she exclaimed, as if at some sudden thought of momentous importance. "I forgot to tell you: I know who you are! What do you think of that? You're Mr. Philo Vance, aren't you? Don't you think I'm terribly smart to know that? I bet you don't know how I found out. I looked at the calling card you gave me this afternoon—and there was your name! That is, Mr. Puttle looked at your card and he said that must be your name. He also got angry for a minute when I told him about the new dress I'm going to get Monday. But then, right away, he was all right again. He said that if you were *that* foolish, it was all right with him, and that you were born every minute. I don't know what he meant. But that's how I found out what your name was." She barely paused for breath.

"And oh! Mr. Puttle told me something else about you. Something *very* exciting. He said you were a sort of detective, and got credit for all the hard work the poor policemen do. Is that *really* true?"

She did not wait for an answer.

"Once my brother wanted to be a policeman, but he didn't. Anyhow, he's hardly big enough to be a real policeman. He's not tall like Mr. Puttle. He's little, like me and George. And I never saw a little policeman, did you? But maybe he could have been a *detective*. I'll bet he never thought of that. Or maybe they don't have little detectives either. Can anybody be a detective if they're too little? Or maybe you don't know."

Vance laughed delightedly, looking into the girl's eyes as if baffled by her entangling digressions.

"I have known some small detectives," he told her.

"Well, anyhow, I guess my brother didn't know about that. Or maybe he didn't want to be a detective. Maybe he just wanted to be a policeman because they wear uniforms... Oh, Mr. Vance! I just thought of something else. I'll bet I know why you're not afraid to be here tonight. They can't arrest a detective! And they can't arrest a policeman, either, can they? If they did, who would they have left to arrest robbers and people like that?... And speaking of my brother, *he's* here tonight, too. He's here *every* night."

"Ah!" murmured Vance. "Where is he sitting?"

"Oh, I don't mean he's here in the dining room," the girl stated naïvely. "He works here."

"Indeed! What does he do?"

"He has a *very* important job."

"Has he been with the *Domdaniel* long?"

"Why, he's been here over six months! That's a *very* long time for my brother. He never seemed to like work very much. I guess he's just a thinker. Anyhow, he says he's never appreciated. And only today he said he was going to try to get his salary raised. But he's afraid the boss here doesn't appreciate him, either."

"What might be the nature of your brother's work?" Vance inquired.

"He works in the kitchen. He's the dishwasher. That's why his job is so important. Just *imagine* if a big café like this didn't have a dishwasher! Wouldn't it be *awful?* Why, you couldn't even get a meal. How could they serve you food if all the dishes were dirty and cluttered up?"

"I must grant your argument," Vance said. "It would be a most distressin' situation. As you say, your brother's job is a most important one. And incidentally, *you* are the most delightfully amazing and the most perfectly natural child I've ever met."

The compliment was evidently lost on her, for she returned at once to the subject of her brother.

"But maybe he's going to quit here tonight. He said he would if he didn't get a raise. But I really don't think he should quit, do you? And I'm going to tell him so!... I bet you don't know where I was going just now."

"Not to the kitchen, I hope."

"Why, you're a *good* detective." The girl's eyes, starry and fluttering, opened wide. "That's where I would have been going, only Philip—that's my brother—said they wouldn't let

me in the kitchen. But I'm going to meet him on the kitchen
stairs. He said I was only putting on airs when I told him I was
coming here tonight. Imagine! He wouldn't believe me. So I
said, 'All right, I'll show you.' And he said, 'If you are in the
Domdaniel you meet me on the landing of the kitchen stairs
at ten o'clock.' So that's where I was going. He was so sure I
wouldn't be here that he said if I showed him I was here by
meeting him, he wouldn't give up his job, no matter if he didn't
get his raise. And I know mother wants him to keep his job. So
you see, everything will work out just fine... Oh, what time is
it, Mr. Vance?"

Vance glanced at his watch.

"It's just five minutes to ten."

The girl rose as suddenly as she had sat down.

"I don't care so much about fooling Philip," she said. "But
I *do* want to make mother happy."

As she hurried toward the distant archway, the lonely Mr.
Burns rose and followed her swiftly into the hall. Almost simul-
taneously the two brushed past the damask draperies of the
doorway, and disappeared from view.

Vance had witnessed the young man's pursuit of Miss
Allen and nodded with benevolent satisfaction.

"Poor unhappy lad," he remarked. "He has grasped his
one fleeting opportunity of speaking alone with his inamo-
rata. I trust he's wise enough not to upbraid her... Ah, well!
Whatever course he pursues, the goddess Aphrodite is already
smiling favorably upon him, though he does not recognize her
beamin' countenance."

I turned my attention indifferently toward the table
where Mirche and Miss Del Marr had been sitting. The singer,
however, had disappeared; and Mirche was scanning the
dining room with complacency. Then he strode down the aisle
toward the main entrance.

As he came to our table he paused with a pompous bow,
to assure himself that all was well with us, and Vance invited
him to join us.

There was nothing particularly distinctive about Daniel Mirche. He was the usual politico-restaurateur type, large and somewhat ostentatious. He was at once aggressive and fawning, with a superficially polished manner. His sparse hair was slightly gray, and his eyes had a peculiar greenish cast.

Vance led the conversation easily along various lines related to Mirche's interest in the café and its management. A discussion of wines and their vintages followed; and it was but a few moments before Vance had launched into one of his favorite topics—namely, the rare cognacs of the west-central Charente Département in France—the *Grande Champagne* and *Petite Champagne* districts and the vineyards around Mainxe and Archiac.

As I glanced idly across the dining room, I noted that Mr. Burns had returned to his table; and soon the young lady herself reappeared in the archway opposite, steering a direct course back to Mr. Puttle. She did not even glance in our direction; and from the crestfallen look of her elf-like face, I assumed that she had failed in her objective.

However, I did not apply myself for long to these reflections. My attention was caught by the unobtrusive and almost cat-like entrance of a slender, exiguous man, who moved, as if loath to attract attention, to a small table in the opposite corner of the room. This table, not far from the one at which the despondent Mr. Burns sat, was already occupied by two men whose backs were to the room; and as the newcomer took the vacant seat facing them, they merely nodded.

My interest in this slight figure was based on the fact that he reminded me of pictures I had seen of one of the most notorious characters of the time, named Owen. There were many unsavory rumors regarding the man, and there had been reports that he was the guiding intelligence—or, as the cliché has it, the "mastermind"—behind certain colossal illegal organizations of gangland. To such an extent was he believed to play a leading, though surreptitious, part in the activities of the underworld that he had earned for himself the sobriquet of "Owl."

There was a remarkable character implicit in his super-refined features. An evil character, to be sure, but one which hinted at vast, and perhaps heroic, potentialities. He had been graduated *cum laude* from a great university; and he recalled to my mind a brilliant painting I had once seen of Robespierre: there was the same smooth and intelligent Machiavellian expression. He was dark of hair and eye, but with a colorless, waxy complexion. The outstanding impression he gave was one of adamantine hardness: one could readily imagine him performing the duties of a Torquemada and smiling thinly as he did so.

(I have described this man at such length because he was to play a vital rôle in the strange record of the case I am here setting down. That night, however, I could not, by the most fantastic flight of my imagination, have associated him in any way with the almost incredible and carefree Gracie Allen. And yet these two divergent characters were soon to cross each other's paths in the most astounding fashion.)

I was just about to dismiss the man from my mind, when I became conscious of an unusual undertone in Vance's voice as he chatted with Mirche. With that peculiarly alert languor I had come to know so well, he was gazing at the table in the far corner where the trio of men sat.

"By the by," he said a bit abruptly to Mirche, "isn't that the famous 'Owl' Owen yonder, near the corner pillar?"

"I am not acquainted with Mr. Owen," Mirche returned suavely. However, he turned slightly with a natural curiosity in the direction which Vance had indicated. "But it well might be," he added after a moment's scrutiny. "He is not unlike the pictures I have seen of Mr. Owen... If I can help you, I might be able to ascertain."

Vance waved the suggestion aside.

"Oh, no—no," he said. "That's awfully good of you, and all that; but it's of no importance, don't y' know."

The members of the orchestra were returning to their places, and Vance pushed back his chair.

"I've had a most pleasant and edifyin' evening," he said to Mirche. "But really, I must be toddlin' now."

Mirche's polite protestations seemed genuine enough as he suggested that we remain at least until after Dixie Del Marr's next number.

"A splendid singer," he added enthusiastically. "And a woman of rare personal charm. She goes on at eleven, and it's almost that now."

But Vance pleaded urgent matters that still required his attention that night, and rose from his chair.

Mirche expressed his profound regrets, and accompanied us to the main entrance where he bade us an effusive good night.

CHAPTER SIX

The Dead Man
(Saturday, May 18; 11 p.m.)

WE DESCENDED THE broad stone steps to the street and turned east. At Seventh Avenue Vance suddenly hailed a taxicab and gave the driver the District Attorney's home address.

"Markham will probably have returned from his round of political chores by this time," he said as we headed downtown. "He'll doubtless twit me unmercifully for my evening's empty adventure; but somehow I felt a strange uneasiness tonight in the spacious confines of the *Domdaniel*, after listening to the Sergeant's uncompliment'ry remarks about the place last night. It was quite the same as of yore. Yet why should the toxiphorous Borgias haunt my mind as I toyed with my *fricandeau* and sipped my *Château Haut-Brion*? Mayhap, as the years roll by, the entanglin' tentacles of suspicion are closin' about my once trustin' nature. *Eheu, eheu!...*"

The cab came to a jerky stop before a small apartment house, and we went at once to the District Attorney's apartment.

Markham, in his smoking jacket and slippers, greeted us with amused surprise.

"Not another wing-sandaled Hermes, I hope."

"Nary a caduceus up my sleeve. Are you being beset by heralds?"

"More or less," returned Markham, with a wry grimace. "The Sergeant here has just brought me a message."

I had not been aware of Heath's presence, but now I saw him standing in the shadow near a window. He came forward with a friendly nod.

"My word, Sergeant," said Vance. "Wherefore?"

"I came on account of that message Mr. Markham was speakin' about, Mr. Vance. A message from Pittsburgh."

"Were the tidings bad?"

"Well, they weren't what you might call good," Heath complained. "Plenty bad, I'd say."

"Indeed?"

"I guess I wasn't so far wrong in the way I figured things last night... Captain Chesholm in Pittsburgh just sent me a report that one of his motorcycle boys had spotted a car running without lights on a back road, and that when the car slowed up for a sharp turn, a guy in the back seat took a couple of shots at him. The car got away, headin' east to the main highway."

"But, Sergeant, why should this bit of desult'ry gun-play in Pennsylvania disturb your even tenor?"

"I'll tell you why." Heath removed the cigar from his mouth. "The officer thought he recognized Benny the Buzzard!"

Vance was unimpressed.

"In the circumst'nces, it could hardly have been a very definite identification."

"That's exactly what I told the Sergeant." Markham nodded approvingly. "During the next few weeks we'll be getting reports that Pellinzi has been seen in every state in the Union."

"Maybe," persisted Heath. "But the way this car was travelin' fits in with my idea perfect. The Buzzard coulda hit New York this morning if he'd come straight from Nomenica. But by circling down to Pennsylvania and coming east from there, he probably figured he would avoid a lot of trouble."

"Personally," Markham said, "I'm convinced the fellow will stay clear of New York." His tone was tantamount to a criticism of the Sergeant's anxiety.

Heath felt the rebuff.

"I hope I haven't bothered you by coming here tonight, Chief. I knew you had a couple of appointments this evening, and I thought you'd still be up."

Markham relented.

"Your coming here was quite all right," he said reassuringly. "I'm always happy to see you, Sergeant. Sit down and help yourself from the decanter... Perhaps Mr. Vance himself is seeking an audience for his information regarding the arch of Mirche's eyebrows and other horrendous details of his sojourn to the *Domdaniel*... How about it, Vance? Have you a bedtime story of goblins with which to regale us?"

Heath had relaxed in a chair and poured himself a drink. Vance, too, reached for his favorite brandy.

"I'm deuced sorry, Markham old dear," he drawled. "I have no fantasies to unfold—not even one about a mysterious fleeing auto. But I shall try to match the Sergeant's inspiration with a yarn of a wood-nymph and a perfume-sniffer; of a xanthous Lorelei who sings from a podium instead of from a rocky crag; of a sleek owner of a caravanserai, and an empty office screened with mysterious grilles; of an ivy-covered postern, and an owl without feathers... Could you bear to hearken to the chantin' of my runes?"

"My resistance is low."

Vance stretched his legs before him.

"Well, *imprimis*," he began, "a most charming and astonishing young woman joined us at our table this evening for a few minutes—a child whose spinning brain, much like a pinwheel, radiated the most colorful sparks, and whose spirit was as guileless as an infant's."

"The wood-nymph of whom you prated in your preamble?"

"Yes—none other. I saw her first this afternoon in a shady nook in Riverdale. And she was at the *Domdaniel* tonight, accompanied by a johnnie named Puttle, with whom she was baiting the true swain of her heart—a Mr. Burns. He, too, was present tonight, but at a distance, and alone—and glowering unhappily."

"Your encounter with her in the afternoon suggests more interesting possibilities," Markham commented listlessly.

"Perhaps you're right, old dear. The fact is, the lady was alone when I intruded into her woodland bower. But she accepted my encroachment quite simply. She even offered to read my palm. It seems that some haruspex named Delpha taught her the lines of the hand—"

"Delpha?" Heath cut in sharply. "You mean the fortune-teller who does business under that phony name?"

"It could be," said Vance. "This Delpha, I gathered, deals in palmistry, astrology, and numerology, and other allied didos. Do you know the seeress, Sergeant?"

"I'll say I do. I know her husband Tony, too. They're connected in some queer way with a lot of wrong guys in the underworld. They're tipsters, jewelry touts—what you might call spies for stickups. But you can't get the goods on 'em. Their name's Tofana; and they run a flashy joint for suckers... 'Delpha'!" he snorted. "Plain Rosie she is to the neighbors. She may get by for a while longer; but I'll nail her some day."

"You positively astound me, Sergeant. I simply can't imagine my sylvan fairy—who, by the by, is a working girl in the In-O-Scent perfume factory on weekdays—having aught to do with the darksome witch of your description."

"*I* can," said Heath. "That's old Rosa Tofana's neatest stall—surrounding herself with young innocents. And while she's putting up the sweet, stainless front, old Tony is probably cooking up some deviltry, or picking pockets, or moll-buzzing, or dope-peddling in another part of town. Slick guy, Tony—can do 'most anything."

"Ah, well," murmured Vance, "we may be speaking of two quite different sibyls, don't y' know. 'Delpha' may be a popular nomenclature with the mystic sorority. Probably a bit of phonetic suggestion for the Delphic oracle..."

"Courage, Vance," Markham put in pleasantly. "Don't let the Sergeant side-track you from your fairy-tale."

"And the most amazin' detail," Vance went on, "was the scent of citron that hung about the pixie. The perfume was mixed especially for her, and was nameless. Most mysterious— eh, what? It had been concocted by the gentleman named Burns—some sort of scent-wizard employed in the same factory she is—who was so annoyed at her apparent deflection to a rival suitor."

Markham smiled wryly.

"I hardly see where the mystery of the situation comes in."

"Nor I," confessed Vance. "But let your massive brain dwell upon the fact that the young lady should have chosen this very night to visit Mirche's hospitium."

"Probably dogged your footsteps from Riverdale till you reached the *Domdaniel.*"

"That, alas! is not the answer. She was already there when I arrived."

"Then perhaps the young lady was hungry."

"I had thought of that." Vance's eyes were twinkling gayly. "Perhaps you've solved the mystery!... But," he went on, "that doesn't account for the further fact that Mirche himself was at the *Domdaniel.*"

"And where else would you have him, pray?... But perhaps you're going to tell me he's the long-lost father of your heroine?"

"No," sighed Vance. "Mirche, I fear, is sublimely unaware of the young lady's very existence. Most annoyin'. And I was trying so hard to build up a diverting yarn for your benefit."

"I appreciate the effort." Markham's cigar needed relighting, and he gave his attention to it. "But tell me what you thought of Mirche. I recall that your main object in going to the *Domdaniel* tonight was to make a closer study of the man."

"Ah, yes." Vance shifted deeper into his chair. "You're always so practical, Markham... Well, I don't like Mirche. A smooth gentleman; but not an admirable one. However, he exerted himself quite earnestly to enchant me. I wonder why... Perhaps he was plotting some shady deed—though he impressed me as being the type who would need another to do his plotting for him. No, not a leader of men, but an unquestioning and able follower. A dark and wicked fellow... Well, there you have the villain of the piece."

"And what shall I do with him?... Your tale is fizzling by the second."

"I fear you're right," admitted Vance. "Let me see... I lovingly inspected Mirche's office; but it was disgustingly void of any wrong. Merely a fair-sized room without a single occupant. And then I gazed fondly at the old door and windows beyond the *porte-cochère*—inside the driveway, y' know. But all my intensive scrutiny yielded nothing of a helpful nature. The ivy round them, however, was most pleasing. English ivy."

"Now you're down to botany," said Markham. "I must say, I prefer the Sergeant's account of the Pittsburgh shooting... But didn't you speak of a Lorelei?"

"Ah, yes. And deuced blonde she was—as becomes a Rhenish siren. Her name, however, has a Gallic ring: Del Marr. A striking Lorelei—more intelligent, I should judge, than Mirche. But there were serious words between her and our Boniface. During a restful intermission of the orchestra they sat together, and I am sure the conversation was not confined to arpeggios and treble clefs and obbligatos. Rather intimate atmosphere. *Liberté, egalité, fraternité—comme ça.* No mere entertainer conversing with her impresario."

"I figured it that way myself, years ago," Heath put in. "Furthermore, she's got a swell car and a chauffeur, too. Her singing don't pay for all that. And I don't like the looks of that chauffeur either: he's a tough mug—looks like he oughta be a bouncer in a saloon."

"At least, Vance," said Markham hopefully, "you have found one potential connection between the almost totally disorganized and unrelated components of your drama. Maybe you can develop your narrative structure with that as a basis."

Vance shook his head despondently.

"No, I fear I am not equal to the task."

"What of the 'owl without feathers' you mentioned a while ago?"

"Ah!" Vance sipped his cognac. "I was referring to the opaque and mysterious Mr. Owen of obnoxious memory and ill repute."

"I see. 'Owl' Owen, eh? I had a vague idea he was basking in the California sunshine. It was rumored some time ago that he was dying—probably of his sins."

"Oh, he was decidedly at the *Domdaniel*, sitting far across the room from me with two other men."

"Those two guys," Heath supplied, "were probably his bodyguard. He don't move without 'em."

"I fear there is no material for you in that quarter, Vance," said Markham. "The F.B.I. were once worried about him; but after an investigation they gave the man a clean bill of health."

"I admit defeat." Vance smiled sadly. "I even tried to lure Mirche into an admission of knowing Owen. But he denied the remotest acquaintance with the man..."

After another hour of random talk we were interrupted by the ringing of the telephone. Markham frowned with annoyance as he answered it; then, putting the receiver down, he turned to Heath.

"For you, Sergeant. It's Hennessey."

Heath, too, was annoyed.

"Sorry, Chief. I didn't leave this number with anyone when I came here."

As he greeted Hennessey over the wire his voice was bellicose. He listened for several minutes, his expression changing rapidly from belligerency to deep puzzlement. Suddenly he bawled into the transmitter: "Hang on a minute!" Holding the receiver at his side, he turned to us.

"It sounds crazy to me, Chief, but Hennessey's calling from the *Domdaniel*, and I gotta see him right away..."

"Splendid!" ejaculated Vance. "Why not have Hennessey come here? I'm sure Mr. Markham wouldn't object."

Markham shot Vance a look of questioning amazement.

"Very well, Sergeant," he grumbled.

Heath quickly put the receiver to his ear again.

"Hey, listen, Hennessey," he barked. "Hop over here to the D. A.'s."

"What might all the excitement be, Sergeant?" asked Vance. "Has Mirche absconded with his own till and eloped with Miss Del Marr?"

"It's damn queer," muttered Heath, ignoring the question. "The boys found a dead guy over at the café."

"I do hope he was found in Mirche's office," Vance said lightly.

"You win." Heath stared at the floor.

"And who might the corpse be?"

"That's what makes it cuckoo. A kitchen helper of some kind that worked there."

"Will that fact help you revive your fizzled tale?" Markham asked Vance.

"My word, no! It blasts my limpin' yarn completely." Vance turned to Heath again. "Did you get the name of the defunct chappie, Sergeant?"

"I didn't pay much attention to it when Hennessey said the guy was just a kitchen mechanic. But it sounded something like Philip Allen."

Vance's eyelids flickered slightly.

"Philip Allen, eh? Most interestin'!"

CHAPTER SEVEN

Queer Coincidences
(Sunday, May 19; 12:45 a.m.)

Hennessey arrived in less than fifteen minutes. He was a heavy-set, serious-minded man with rugged features and an awkward manner.

Heath went directly to the point.

"Tell your story, Hennessey. Then I'll ask questions. But first I want to know why you called me here at this time of night."

"Hell, Sergeant!" Hennessey returned. "I'd been trying for over an hour to get hold of you. I knew you had some idea about Mr. Markham and the *Domdaniel*, and I figured you'd want to know about an unexpected death there. So I called your home and a lot of other places I thought you might be at. No dice. Then I took a chance and called you here. I didn't want you bawling me out tomorrow."

"Well, what do you know?" grumbled Heath.

"The story sounds cockeyed, Sergeant, but along about eleven o'clock I saw Mr. Vance come out of the café. Earlier, I'd seen him monkeying around Mirche's office—"

"At eight," Vance put in with a smile.

Hennessey took out his notebook and turned a few pages. "Seven fifty-six, Mr. Vance."

"My word, what meticulous observation!"

Hennessey grinned.

"Well, about fifteen or twenty minutes after Mr. Vance left, two men from the Bureau drives up with Doc Mendel;[*] and the three of 'em go in Mirche's office. It looked like funny business to me, so I left Burke on watch, and Snitkin and I went to see what it was all about. Just as we was hopping up the steps, Mirche himself comes hurrying down the terrace, all excited, and busts past us into the office. I guess the doorman—you know him: Joe Hanley—musta told him that somethin' queer was goin' on..."

"Never mind guessing."

"All right," Hennessey continued. "Inside the office was a guy in a black suit lying all bunched up on the floor, halfway under the desk. Mirche went over to him, sort of staggerin' and dead-white himself. He leaned close over the guy, alongside the doc who was opening the fellow's shirt and putting one of those ear-trumpets on his chest..."

"A stethoscope! My word!" Vance looked at Markham. "I didn't know an official Æsculapius ever carried one of those trusty instruments."

"They don't, as a rule," said Markham. "Mendel's a young fellow; just been appointed to the staff; and I wouldn't be surprised if he carries a sphygmomanometer around with him, and his diploma, too."

"Go on, Hennessey," Heath growled. "Then what?"

"Guilfoyle asked Mirche who the guy was. I don't know whether it was before or after Mirche answered the question;

---

*   One of the Assistant Medical Examiners of New York.

but anyhow along about then Dixie Del Marr came rushing in. And Mirche says, husky-like, it was one of his dishwashers at the café—a fellow named Philip Allen. I coulda told Guilfoyle that much. I knew Allen, and had seen him myself that afternoon. Then Guilfoyle asks Mirche what the fellow was doing in the office, and where he lived, and what Mirche knew about his being dead. The old toad says he don't know nothing about the dead guy, or how he come to be there, or where he lives—that it was all a mystery to him. And he sure looked the part."

"You're sure he wasn't puttin' one over on you?" asked Heath suspiciously.

"Huh! Not me," Hennessey asserted. "A guy can't look that jolted and not mean it."

"What happened then?"

Hennessey continued more rapidly.

"The doc went on examining the man, lifting up his eyelids, looking down his throat, moving his legs and arms— the regular rigamarole. And while he was busy monkeying with the guy, this Dixie Del Marr opens the door of a built-in closet and brings out a ledger. She turns a few pages, then says: 'Here it is, Dan'—meanin' Mirche. 'Philip Allen lives at 198 East 37th Street—with his mother.' "

Markham looked up and turned to Vance.

"I see that your not too profound deduction is being mildly substantiated. Your blonde Lorelei is evidently Mirche's bookkeeper."

Hennessey was impatient at the interruption.

"Guilfoyle then asked the doc what the fellow had died of. The doc had the body on its face now, and when he looked round at Guilfoyle you'da thought he'd never seen a corpse before. 'I don't know,' he said. 'He might have died a natural death, but I can't tell with this much of an examination. He's got some burns on his lips, and his throat don't look so hot'—or words to that effect. 'You'll have to get him down to the morgue for a post-mortem.' He didn't even seem to know how long the guy was dead."

"What about the Del Marr woman?" prompted Heath.

"She put the book back and sat down in a chair looking hard and indifferent, until Mirche sent her back to the café."

"So you sent the body down to the morgue." Heath was puffing gloomily on his cigar.

"That's right, Sergeant. Guilfoyle took care of calling for the buggy. He and the other man from the Bureau, Sullivan, stayed on the job... It's a dumb enough story, but I know you've always been leery about this fellow Mirche—especially now with the Buzzard on the loose."

Heath furrowed his brow and fixed Hennessey with a cold stare.

"All right!" he bellowed. "Who went in that office after Mr. Vance arrived there at eight?"

"Oh, that's easy." The officer laughed mirthlessly. "The Del Marr woman went in around eight-thirty and come right out again. Then, a little while later, the doorman sauntered down, and he went in too. But I figure that ain't nothing unusual for him: I reckon Hanley just sneaked in for a snifter, for he came out rubbing his coat sleeve across his mouth..."

"What time was all this?" asked Heath.

"Early in the evening—within an hour after Mr. Vance had been there."

"I suppose you checked if either of 'em saw the dead guy?"

"Sure I did. But neither one of 'em saw him. The doorman went in after the Del Marr woman did; and you can bet your life that if there'd been a corpse in there, Hanley would have let out a holler. He's a right guy, Sergeant."

"Sure; I've known Joe Hanley plenty long." Heath thought a moment. "All of that don't add up... But here's something you can tell me: What time did you take your nap tonight?"

The import of Heath's question suddenly dawned on me.

"Honest to God, Sergeant, I didn't take any nap. But—so help me!—I never saw that guy Allen go into the office."

"Huh!" A world of sarcasm was in the Sergeant's grunt. "You didn't go to sleep, but Allen slips into the office, has a

heart attack, or somethin', and folds up under Mirche's desk!—
That's a hot one for the record!"

Hennessey turned a vivid red.

"I—I don't blame you for squawking, Sergeant. But, on
the level, I didn't look away from that door for a split second—"

"Then this guy just made himself invisible and wished
himself in there. Or maybe he came down the chimney like
Santa Claus—if there'd been a chimney." The Sergeant's irony
seemed unnecessarily brutal.

"I say, Sergeant," Vance put in. "The real object of
Hennessey's vigil, y' know, was to keep an eye open for Benny
Pellinzi. You certainly didn't put three husky gentlemen in the
rooming-house to keep track of a poor dishwasher."

Heath took up another phase of the problem.

"Who put in the call to Headquarters, Hennessey?"

"That's another funny one, Sergeant. The call came
through in the regular way at ten-fifty—not more'n ten minutes
or so after you'd left. It was a woman who phoned. She wouldn't
give her name; played mysterious and hung up."

"Yeah. *I'll* say that's funny... Mighta been this Del Marr
wren."

"I thought of her myself, and asked her about it. But she
seemed as ignorant about it as Mirche did. But it coulda been
one of the old crones that work around the kitchen. A lot of
the help comes and goes through that driveway alongside the
office. And if one of 'em should happen to get nosy, they could
stretch up and look through the window."

"What about the office building that adjoins the driveway?"
Vance asked.

Heath answered the question.

"There's no windows there, sir. A solid brick wall for the
first three floors..."

Vance's cigarette had burnt out, and he lighted a fresh one.

"Puttin' it all together," he commented, "it doesn't look very
promisin' for a mysterious crime. Very sad. I had such lofty hopes
when Hennessey phoned at this more or less witchin' hour."

"I gotta admit," Heath confessed, "I can't get hold of anything special in Hennessey's report, myself... But there's something else I'd like to know." He turned back to Hennessey. "You say you knew this dishwasher, Allen, and saw him earlier in the day. What about that?"

"The way I happen to know him," returned the officer, "is that he came running outa the driveway one night last winter, about three in the morning, and damn near knocked me down. I grabbed him and checked him up with Hanley. Then I turned him loose... This afternoon I seen him buzzing round Mirche's office. He went in and out three or four times between lunch and five o'clock. Then, around six, when Mirche had got there, he went in again and stayed about ten minutes that time. When he came out, that was the last I seen of him."

"Where did he go?"

"How should *I* know? I ain't no mind-reader. He didn't go back to the kitchen, if that's what you want to know. He just went on down the street."

"You sure it was Allen you saw?" the Sergeant asked dispiritedly.

"I'll say I'm sure!" Hennessey laughed. "But it's damn funny you should ask me that. The first time I seen Allen this afternoon, I got the screwy idea it coulda been Benny the Buzzard: they're both about the same size, with the same round pasty-looking face. And Allen had on a plain black suit, like I told you—which is the way the Buzzard mighta dressed if he'd been sneaking back here and didn't want to be spotted too easy. You remember the loud natty get-ups he wore in the old days. Anyhow, I thought I'd make sure. I knew I was being dumb, but I went over and said hello to the fellow. It was Allen, all right. He told me he was hanging around to get a raise out of old Mirche. Swell chance!"

Heath scratched his head.

"Anything else about this fellow Allen come to you?"

"I was just thinking," Hennessey said. "Yeah...he met a guy about the middle of the afternoon—around four o'clock.

He was a little fellow like Allen. They met just west of the café, and pretty soon they got into an argument. It looked like they was going to come to blows any minute. But I didn't pay much attention to 'em; and finally this guy went on his way... Anything else on your mind, Sergeant?"

Vance beckoned Heath to one side and spoke a few whispered words to him. At length the Sergeant shrugged his shoulders and nodded. Then he turned again to Hennessey.

"That's all," he said. "Go home and get some *more* sleep. But be back on the job at noon."

When Hennessey had gone, Markham, noting a sudden change in Vance's manner, frowned and leaned forward.

"What's on your mind, Vance?" he asked.

"Hennessey's tale. Y' know, in my fairy-story this evening, I didn't mention the name of the wood-nymph. The name is Gracie Allen. And Philip Allen is her brother. She informed me quite frankly he was a dishwasher at the *Domdaniel*. She even told me he was going to beard Mirche in his den this afternoon to petition for an increased stipend. And when Miss Allen stopped at my table tonight, she was on her way to meet her brother somewhere in the recesses of the café."

Markham leaned back again with a short laugh.

"Maybe you can fit all that into the fantasy you were spinning earlier."

"As you say, old dear." Vance was no longer in a jesting mood. "I'm certainly going to try. I don't fancy so many irrelevant things happening in one place and at one time. Something must be holding them together. At any rate, I'm in no mood to emulate Pepys and betake myself home and to bed."

Vance walked the length of the room and back, his head down; then he came to an abrupt stop, and smiled with an abashed, yet determined, earnestness.

"See here, Markham," he said; "I admit my ideas are dashed vague, and that the charmin' little witch in Riverdale may have cast a spell over me. But I feel compelled to find out what I can about Philip Allen's untimely death, and maybe

lessen the shock for the young lady. And I need your helpin'
hand. Wouldst humor my vagaries once more?"

Markham sighed with resignation.

"Anything to get rid of you at this ungodly hour."

"Feelin' thus, give me the Allen case instanter, to play with
as I jolly well please—with the doughty Sergeant at my side, of
course."

Markham hesitated.

"How do you feel about this, Sergeant?"

"If Mr. Vance has got some fancy ideas," returned Heath
vigorously, "I'd just as soon string along with him."

"All right, Sergeant, go ahead and humor our amateur
playwright." Then Markham turned back to Vance. "And as for
you," he said with good-natured effrontery, "I think you're a
raving maniac."

"Granted," said Vance. "No *de lunatic inquirendo* writ
necess'ry."

CHAPTER EIGHT

At the Mortuary
(Sunday, May 19; 1:30 a.m.)

VANCE AND HEATH and I went first to Vance's apartment. Here, while Vance changed from evening clothes to a sack suit, Heath did some necessary telephoning.

He questioned Guilfoyle at some length regarding any pertinent details Hennessey might have omitted, and gave orders for Sullivan to remain at the *Domdaniel* till noon the next day. He then called Doctor Mendel. I gathered, both from his expression and the questions he put, that Heath was puzzled and annoyed by the information he was getting from the young doctor. When Vance rejoined us, the Sergeant was apparently still pondering the matter.

"This thing," he said, "is beginning to look even more cuckoo than Hennessey's story sounded. Doc Mendel still thinks Allen mighta died natural; but he found a lot of nutty evidence that there coulda been dirty work. He's passing the buck, and got the body to the morgue quick, where Doremus* will do the autopsy. Mendel don't want any part of it. When I asked him what time he thought the fellow died, he stalled around about *rigor mortis* and some sort of spasm."

"Cadaveric spasm," supplied Vance.

"Yeah, that's it. And then he began mumbling that there's lots of things in medicine that ain't known yet—is he tellin' me!"

"Sounds most familiar, don't y' know," sighed Vance. "But, in the meantime, what about Mrs. Allen?"

"Sure; she's gotta be notified. Thought I'd send Martin— he's smooth and easy."

"No—oh, no, Sergeant," said Vance. "I could bear to see the lady myself. *You* take on the chore, and I'll stagger along."

"All right, sir." The Sergeant cocked his eye and grinned. "You asked for it—and it's *your* case. Anyhow, this identification job won't take long."

We found Mrs. Allen's residence in East 37th Street a modest place—an old brownstone-front structure that had been divided into small apartments. Mrs. Allen herself answered our ring. She was fully dressed, and all the lights were on in the plainly furnished room.

She was a frail, mouse-like person who seemed much older than I had expected Miss Allen's mother to be. There was a softness and vagueness in her expression—almost a wistful- ness—like that of a woman who had grown old before her time either through sudden sorrow or prolonged hardships.

She appeared highly nervous and frightened by our pres- ence at the door; but when the Sergeant told her who he was, she straightway invited us in. She sat down rigidly as if to steel herself against some blow. Her hands were clasped so tightly that the knuckles showed white.

Heath cleared his throat. For all his hardness of nature, he appeared peculiarly sympathetic.

---

*   *Doctor Emanuel Doremus, Chief Medical Examiner of New York.*

"You're Mrs. Allen," he began. It was half question and half statement.

The woman nodded shakily.

"You got a son named Philip?"

She merely nodded again; but the pupils of her eyes dilated.

Heath shifted his weight and looked about him for a moment. His face softened perceptibly. Only once before had I seen the Sergeant so deeply moved: that was when he gazed into the abandoned closet at the still form of little Madeleine Moffat, during his investigation of the Bishop murder case.*

"You're sitting up pretty late, aren't you, Mrs. Allen?" he asked, as if he had found no words as yet to soften the blow.

"Yes, Mr. Officer," the woman said, in a small tremulous voice. "I always sit up and wait for my daughter when she's out. But I don't mind."

Heath nodded and, with a sudden rush of words, came to the point.

"Well, I'm sorry, but I got bad news for you," he blurted. "Your son Philip's met with an accident." He paused for several moments. "Yes, Mrs. Allen, I gotta tell you—he's dead. He was found tonight at the café where he works."

The woman clutched at her chair. Her eyes opened wide; and her body swayed a little. Vance went quickly to her and, taking her by the shoulders, steadied her.

"Oh, my poor boy!" she moaned several times. Then she looked from one to the other of us as if dazed. "Tell me what happened."

"We don't quite know, madam," Vance said softly.

"But when," she asked in a colorless tone, "—when did this happen?"

"We got the call about eleven o'clock tonight," Heath told her.

"I—I don't know what to do." She looked up appealingly. "Will you take me to him?"

---

*   "*The Bishop Murder Case*" (*Scribners, 1929*).

"That's just what we came here for, Mrs. Allen. We want you to come with us—for only a few minutes—a little ways downtown—and identify him. Mr. Mirche has already done that, of course; but just for the records we got to ask you to do it too. Then we can straighten everything out..."

Vance now spoke to the woman.

"I know it's a frightfully sad errand for you, Mrs. Allen. But, as the Sergeant explained, it is a necess'ry matter of form; and it will make things easier for you and your daughter later on. You'll try to be brave, won't you?"

She nodded vaguely.

"Yes, I've got to be brave for Gracie's sake."

I could not but admire the fortitude of this frail woman, and when she got up with determination to put on her hat and cape, my admiration for her rose even higher.

"I'll only stop to leave a note for my daughter," she said apologetically, when she was ready to go. "She would worry so if she came home and I wasn't here."

We waited while she found a piece of paper. Vance offered her his pencil. Then, with an unsteady hand, she wrote a few words, and left the paper in full view on the table.

On the way downtown the woman did not speak, but listened meekly to the Sergeant's instructions and suggestions.

When we passed through the elevator door of the city's mortuary in 29th Street, she put her hands to her face and half breathed a few words, as if in prayer, adding in a louder tone, "Oh, my poor Philip! He was such a good boy at heart."

Heath took her protectingly by the arm, and led her solicitously into the bare basement room. The episode did not prove as gruesome as I had pictured it beforehand. Mrs. Allen's harrowing experience was over the moment Heath halted her steps before the still form that had been wheeled out on a slab from its crypt. Her ordeal was terminated quickly and in merciful fashion.

After one momentary glance, she turned away with a stifled sob and collapsed in a crumpled heap.

The Sergeant, who had been watching the woman closely from the time we had stepped out of the elevator, took her up swiftly in his arms, and carried her into the dimly lighted reception room, where he placed her on a wicker sofa. Her face was colorless, and her breathing shallow; but after a few minutes she began to move feebly. Then, with the rush of blood to the cheeks and moisture to the skin, which accompanies the reaction from a faint, came a flood of tears.

When she had wept freely for a moment or two, Heath pulled up a chair and sat down facing her.

"I know, Mrs. Allen," he said, "this must be mighty painful for you, but you know we got to be careful in cases like this. It's the law. We couldn't afford to make any mistakes about it. And you wouldn't want us to, would you?"

"Oh, that would be terrible." Her hand moved slowly across her eyes, as if to blot out some terrifying vision.

"Sure...I know," mumbled the Sergeant. "That's why you got to forgive us for being sort of heartless."

"When," she asked, like one who had not heard his words, "—when will the poor boy—?"

"That's another thing I got to tell you, Mrs. Allen." Heath interrupted her unfinished query. "You see, we ain't going to be able to let you take your son right away. The doctor ain't sure just what he died of; and we got to make sure. It's as much for your sake as it is for ours. So we got to keep him for a day— maybe two days."

She moved her head up and down sadly.

"I know what you mean," she said. "I once had a nephew who died in a hospital..." She left the sentence unfinished, and added: "I know I can trust you."

"Yes, Mrs. Allen," Vance assured her. "The Sergeant won't take any longer than is necess'ry. These matters must be handled legally and carefully. I promise to let you know myself—the very moment the matter is settled... I'll also be very glad to help you and your daughter in any other way I can."

The woman turned slowly to Vance and studied him for a moment. A look of confidence and appeal came into her eyes.

"It's my daughter," she began softly. "I want to ask you something for her sake. It will mean so much to her, and to me, just now. Please—*please*—don't tell my daughter about Philip yet. Not till she has to know—and then I want to tell her myself... She would worry about things which maybe aren't true at all. She has a lot of imagination—inherited from me, I guess. Why not let her have one more day, or maybe two more days, of happiness? Just until you make sure?"

It was obvious the woman's request was actuated by a suspicion that her son had not died a natural death; and she feared a similar doubt might haunt the daughter too.

"But, Mrs. Allen," Vance asked, "if we keep this matter quiet for a time, how would you account to your daughter for her brother's absence? Surely, she would be concerned about that."

Mrs. Allen shook her head.

"No. Philip stays away from home often, sometimes for days at a time. Only today he said he might give up his job at the café and maybe leave the city. No, Gracie won't suspect anything."

Vance looked interrogatively at Heath.

"I believe, Sergeant," he said, "that it would be both humane and wise to comply with Mrs. Allen's wishes."

Heath nodded vigorously.

"Yes, so do I, Mr. Vance. I think it can be managed."

An understanding look passed between the two, and then Vance addressed Mrs. Allen again.

"We will be very happy to make you that promise, madam."

"And there will be nothing about it in the papers?" she asked tentatively.

"I think that, too, can be arranged," Vance said.

"Thank you," said Mrs. Allen simply.

Just then an attendant came into the room and motioned to the Sergeant, who rose and walked across to him. A few words passed between them, and together they walked out through a side door. A few minutes later the Sergeant returned, slipping something into his pocket.

Mrs. Allen had now somewhat recovered her composure; and as the Sergeant rejoined us, he smiled at her encouragingly.

"I guess we can be taking you home now."

We drove Mrs. Allen back to her little apartment, and bade her good night.

A few minutes later the three of us were in Vance's library. It was just half-past two in the morning.

"A strange little woman," Vance murmured, as he poured a nightcap of brandy for each of us. "Remarkably brave, too. I really had no anxiety about leaving her alone in her home. She rallied better than I thought she would after the distressing experience."

"I've known a lot of little women like that," commented Heath, "who could take it better than a big husky bruiser."

"Yes, quite... I wonder if her effort to spare her daughter will be as successful as she hopes. Gracie Allen is no ordin'ry young woman—she's astute, despite her astonishin' and flighty vivacity."

"The old lady sure made it easy for us," the Sergeant remarked.

Vance nodded as he sipped his brandy.

"Exactly. That's just what I had in mind, Sergeant. We need have no concern about interference until Doremus' post-mortem report is completed. Mrs. Allen will surely not press us, for I imagine she will be grateful for any additional respite for her daughter. And Mirche will certainly find it advantageous to keep his own counsel—he's not eager for any unsav'ry publicity in connection with the *Domdaniel*... Will you do all you can to keep the case hushed up as long as possible, Sergeant?"

"At last you're asking me to do something easy," grinned Heath. "I'll tell the boys at the Bureau to pipe down; and you can go on runnin' round and asking questions for a couple of days without anyone nagging at you."

Vance smiled languidly, but he was still troubled.

Heath finished his brandy, and lighted a long black cigar.

"By the way, Mr. Vance, here's something that might interest you." He reached into his coat pocket and drew out a small wooden cigarette case, peculiarly grained and with alternating squares of light and dark lacquer, giving it a distinctive checkerboard design. "I found it among Allen's belongings at the morgue."

"But why, my dear Sergeant, should it interest me?"

"Well, I don't exactly know, sir." Heath was almost apologetic. "But I know you got ideas about tonight that I ain't got."

"But there's nothing extr'ordin'ry in the fact that the young chap smoked cigarettes."

"It ain't that, sir." Heath opened the case and pointed to one inside corner of the lid. "There's a name burnt in the wood there—looks like a amateur job. And, it so happens, the name is 'George'. That ain't the dead fellow's name."

Vance's expression changed suddenly. He leaned forward and, taking the cigarette case from Heath, looked at the crudely burnt lettering.

"Things shouldn't happen this way—really, y' know, they shouldn't, Sergeant. Gracie Allen's true-love is named George. George Burns, to be precise. The same johnnie I mentioned earlier at Mr. Markham's. And this Mr. Burns was at the *Domdaniel* tonight. And so was Gracie. And her flashy escort, Mr. Puttle. And Philip Allen. And the oleaginous Mirche. And the undecipherable Dixie Del Marr. And the mysterious 'Owl' Owen. And the ominous shadow of a buzzard."

"What do you make of it, Mr. Vance?"

"Sergeant—oh, my Sergeant!" sighed Vance. "What could anyone make of it? Precisely nothing. That's why I'm aging so perceptibly before your very eyes. That's why my locks are turning white."

"How do you think that cigarette case got in Philip Allen's pocket, Mr. Vance?" Heath held stubbornly to his problem.

"Stop torturing me!" Vance pleaded.

Heath took the cigarette case, snapped it shut, and returned it to his pocket.

"I'm going to find out," he said with determination. "If Philip Allen didn't die a natural death, and if this gimmick belongs to the Burns guy, I'll sweat the truth out of him if I got to invent a new way to do it... This thing's getting *me* down, too, Mr. Vance. None of it makes sense, sir; and I don't like anything that don't make sense... I'll find the baby—and I'll find him tonight. The *Domdaniel's* closed by now, so maybe he went home—if he's got a home. I'll tackle the factory first. What did you say that name was, sir?"

"The In-O-Scent Corporation," smiled Vance. "Rather discouragin' name with which to start your quest for a suspect—eh, what, Sergeant? Somehow I rather hope the name'll prove symbolic."

"You're too deep for me, sir," Heath complained, moving toward the door. "All I gotta worry about right now is finding that guy Burns."

"Well, Sergeant, when you do corner Mr. Burns, we can either eliminate one part of the puzzle, or else put it some place where it will fit." He drew a deep sigh. "I'll be waiting for your scented tidings in the morning."

CHAPTER NINE

Held On Suspicion
(Sunday, May 19; 10:30 a.m.)

IT WAS ALMOST half-past ten Sunday morning when Heath called at Vance's apartment. Vance had risen only shortly before and was sitting in the library, robed in a mandarin dressing gown, having his usual scant breakfast of thick Turkish coffee. He had just lighted his second cigarette when the Sergeant was ushered in, looking somewhat weary but triumphant.

"At last I've got him!" he announced, without pausing for salutations.

"My word, Sergeant!" Vance greeted him. "Seat yourself and relax. You should have some strengthenin' coffee. No doubt you're referring to Burns. But don't tell me you were round and about all night on your quest."

Heath sat down heavily.

"I was round and about plenty. And if you don't mind, Mr. Vance, would you put a little something else in that coffee? I need pickin' up."

Vance complied, smiling.

"Tell me about your nocturnal wanderin's, Sergeant."

"Well, the fact is, sir, I ain't exactly got him yet," Heath amended; "but I'm expecting a phone call here any minute from Emery—I've got him watching Mrs. Allen's house, and—"

"Mrs. Allen's house?"

"Yeah! That's where the guy's headin' for."

"The affair sounds frightfully complicated, don't y' know."

"It wasn't so complicated, Mr. Vance," answered Heath. "It was just a damn nuisance... When I left here last night, I went down to the In-O-Scent factory, and got hold of the night watchman. He let himself into the office with his pass-key, and found the book of employees, and showed me Burns' name with the address of a second-rate hotel only a few blocks away. So I takes it easy and goes over there. But it seems Burns has already been in, changed his clothes, and gone out again. The night clerk gives me this information. Then I shows him the cigarette case. And that's where I run into a piece of luck. The fellow's ready to swear Burns has got one just like it—Burns often stops to gabble with him when he gets in late."

"And," put in Vance, "most likely offers the other a cigarette during the gay banter."

"That's it, sir... Then I calls Emery, down at the Bureau, to come up and wait around, in case this Burns figures on coming back. After he gets there I goes home to grab a couple of hours' sleep."

"And did your Cerberus interrupt your slumbers with news of the missing perfume-sniffer?"

"No. Burns didn't show up at his hotel again. So at eight o'clock I goes back to the hotel myself to see what else I can get outa the night clerk. And it seems that him an' Burns an' two other guys, friends of Burns, sometimes sits around playing cards in the lobby at night. One of 'em lives across the street, but this guy says he ain't seen Burns for days. But he tells me to try the other fellow, named Robbin, out in Brooklyn, as Burns often spends a night at Robbin's place—especially Saturday night. So I beats it out to Brooklyn. I don't phone Robbin's place, because I don't wanta give Burns any tip-off. It takes me over an hour to locate the house, which is half a dozen blocks off the main line, over to hell-and-gone in Bensonhurst."

"What a beastly matutinal odyssey, Sergeant!" Vance shuddered dolefully. "And what befell when you came at last to the hut of Eumæus?"

"The guy's name is Robbin, like I told you. And he don't live in a hut… Well, I asked him about Burns, and he told me Burns had come out there at three o'clock this morning, saying he wasn't feeling so hot and wanted company. Robbin also told me Burns was nervous and didn't sleep very good. He was up early and had beat it before I got there… What do you make of that, Mr. Vance?"

"Sounds very much like florescent love in a state of suspense," said Vance. "Ah, the sweet cruelty of woman!"

"I don't know what you're getting at, sir," replied the Sergeant, "but it sounds like a guilty conscience to me. Especially with Burns not staying home—running away, so to speak—and hiding out in the wilds of Bensonhurst… Anyhow, when I showed Robbin the cigarette case, he knew it right away. He couldn't remember for sure if Burns had it on him last night. I asked Robbin if he had any idea where Burns went. Then he just laughed and said he *knew* where Burns went, but that he wouldn't be there till eleven o'clock. So, seeing that he couldn't have got back to New York yet, I telephones to Emery at Burns' hotel, to get on the job watching her house…"

"Mrs. Allen's house?"

"Yeah. That's where Robbin said Burns would be at eleven o'clock. And he didn't have any doubts about it either. I figured this was reasonable. You yourself, Mr. Vance, told me Burns was the girl's boyfriend; and he mighta had an idea of getting some kind of help from her and the old lady before they got wise to him. So I hops back here to New York in a hurry. And here I am, reportin' to you and waitin' for Emery's phone call."

"Extr'ordin'ry!" murmured Vance. "What zeal! You've fitted many facts together, and not unskilfully, while I merely slumbered. And I presume you will fare forth when you get Emery's summons and chivy young Burns no end."

"I'll say I will!" Then the Sergeant added: "I'm beginning to think you actually had an idea last night at the D. A.'s."

"I wonder... In any event, I'm going along with you, Sergeant." And Vance started for the door of his dressing room.

"I thought you'd be wanting to go, sir. But there's one thing I got to ask you: let me handle this my own way."

"Oh, by all means, Sergeant." And Vance went from the library.

He had just returned to the room, fully dressed, when the telephone rang. Heath jumped from his chair and had the receiver at his ear before Currie, Vance's old valet and major-domo, could reach the instrument.

It was the awaited call from Emery, and after listening for a brief moment, Heath responded eagerly.

"Right! I'll be there in five minutes." He slammed down the receiver and, rubbing his hands together in satisfaction, made for the door. "Come on, Mr. Vance. We're getting places at last..."

As we turned the corner from Lexington Avenue, we saw Emery lounging across the street from Mrs. Allen's house. He took a few steps toward us and nodded significantly.

Heath grunted his acknowledgment, and gave Emery orders to follow us inside.

It was Gracie Allen who answered our ring this time. She caught sight of Vance immediately and threw up her hands in exuberant delight.

"Oh, hello, Mr. Vance! How *wonderful!*" she called out musically, seeming almost to flutter. "How did you find out where I live? You must be an *awfully* smart detective..."

As she noticed the grim presence of the two other men, she broke off abruptly.

"These gentlemen are police officers, Miss Allen," Vance told her, "and we have come to—"

"Oh! They *caught* you, didn't they!" she exclaimed in dismay. "Isn't that terrible!" Her eyes grew large. "But honest, Mr. Vance, I didn't tell on you. I wouldn't do such a thing— *really* I wouldn't. Not after I gave you my promise..."

Heath and Emery were brushing past her into the room, and Vance held up his hand to her.

"Please, my dear," he said earnestly. "Just a moment. We've come here about quite a different matter."

She stepped back from him, awed by his serious manner; and Vance followed the two officers into the room.

On a sofa against the opposite wall sat young George Burns, obviously annoyed by our intrusion. Heath had already crossed rapidly to him.

"Your name's George Burns, ain't it?" he asked gruffly.

"It always has been," Burns returned with surly resentment. "Who wants to know?"

"Wise guy, eh?" Heath fumbled in his pockets, and then asked in a conciliatory tone. "Got a cigarette, Burns?"

Burns automatically brought out a package of cigarettes.

"What!" exclaimed the Sergeant. "Ain't you got a cigarette case?"

"Why, of course, he has!" stated Gracie Allen loftily. "I gave him one myself last Christmas—a real pretty one, like a checkerboard—"

Vance silenced her with an arresting gesture.

"Yes," admitted Burns, "I did have one; but I—I lost it yesterday." He seemed nonplused by the line of questioning.

"Maybe this is it." Heath spoke with menacing emphasis, as he shoved the little cigarette case under Burns' nose.

Burns, startled and intimidated, nodded weakly. Taking the case, he held it against his nostrils and sniffed at it several times. Then he looked up at the Sergeant.

"Kiss Me Quick!"

"What!" exploded Heath.

"Oh," mumbled Burns, embarrassed. "That's just the name of a well-known handkerchief perfume. The formula calls for cassie, jonquille, civet, citronella—"

"Oh, and I know what else," supplied Miss Allen eagerly. "Jasmine and tuberose—"

Burns was exasperated.

"You're thinking of *Leap Year**..."

"Say, listen!" bawled Heath. "What's going on here, anyhow?"

Vance was laughing quietly to himself.

The Sergeant snatched the cigarette case from Burns, and put it back into his pocket.

"Where did you lose that case yesterday?"

Burns fidgeted.

"I—I didn't exactly lose it. I just—well, I just sort of lent it to somebody."

"So! Lending Christmas presents from your best girl, was you?"

"Well, I didn't exactly lend it, either." Burns became confused. "I met a fellow and offered him a cigarette. Then we got in a little argument; and I guess he just forgot..."

"Sure! He just walked off with the case," retorted Heath with mammoth sarcasm. "And you forgot to ask him for it, and let him keep it—as a nice little present from you to him. That's swell!... Who was the fellow?"

Burns squirmed.

"Well—if you must know—it was Miss Allen's brother."

"Sure it was! You're pretty foxy, ain't you?" Then a new idea suddenly smote the Sergeant. "That musta been up near the *Domdaniel* café. Along about four o'clock in the afternoon."

"How did *you* know?" Burns asked, amazed.

"*I'm* asking the questions," snapped Heath. "And it wasn't just a *little* argument like you said. It came pretty near being a

---

*   *Both* Kiss Me Quick *and* Leap Year Bouquet *are popular "fancy" concentrates. Full descriptions and recipes may be found in Poucher's standard work, "Perfumes, Cosmetics and Soaps."*

fist-fight, didn't it? You were good and sore about something, weren't you?"

Burns stared helplessly at the Sergeant, and then at Gracie Allen.

"Oh, goodness, George!" the girl exclaimed. "Were you and Philip squabbling again? You're just a pair of squabs."

Heath gritted his teeth.

"You keep outa this, Baby-doll."

"Oooo!" The girl giggled coyly. "That's what Mr. Puttle called me last night."

Heath turned back to Burns in disgust.

"What were you and Allen fighting about?"

The man rolled his eyes vaguely, as if afraid to answer yet afraid not to answer. Finally he stammered:

"It was about Gracie—Miss Allen. Philip doesn't seem to—like me. He told me to keep away from—well, away from here. And then he said I didn't know how to dress—that I didn't have the style of this *Mister* Puttle..."

"Well, *I* got something to tell you, too. And it's nifty—"

Vance quickly tapped the Sergeant on the shoulder and whispered something to him.

Heath drew himself up and, turning round, pointed at the girl.

"You go in the other room, Miss. I got something to say to this young man alone—get me?—*alone.*"

"That's right, Gracie." I was surprised to hear Mrs. Allen's quiet voice. She was standing timidly wedged in a small opening between the sliding doors at the rear of the room. How long she had been there I did not know. "You come with me, Gracie, and leave these gentlemen with George."

The girl did not demur; and she and her mother went into the rear room, drawing the doors together behind them.

"And now for the bad news, young fellow," Heath resumed, stepping threateningly toward the dumbfounded Burns. But again Vance interrupted him.

"Just a moment, Sergeant. Why, Mr. Burns, were you so surprised just now at the scent on your cigarette case?"

"I don't—I don't know, exactly." Burns frowned. "It's not a usual scent; I haven't come across it for a long time. But at the café last night, I did notice it quite strong at the entrance in the front hall, just as I was going into the dining room."

"Who was wearing it?"

"Oh, I couldn't possibly know that—there were so many people standing around."

Vance seemed satisfied and, with a gesture, turned the young man back to the Sergeant.

"Well, here's the bad news," Heath barked abusively at Burns. "We found a dead guy last night—and that cigarette case of yours was in his pocket."

Burns' head came up with a jerk, and a stunned, frightened light came into his eyes.

"My God!" he breathed. "Who—who was it?"

Heath grinned cruelly.

"I just can't imagine. Maybe *you* can guess."

"It wasn't—Philip!" Burns gasped. "Oh, my God!... I know he isn't here today. But he went out of town—honest to God, he did. He told me yesterday he was going."

"You ain't quite smart enough, though you was pretty foxy tryin' to drag someone else in it with that hocus-pocus about perfume." Heath paused, and then reached a sudden decision. He made a curt sign to Emery. "We're taking this baby along with us," he announced. "We'll keep him where we can reach him easy."

Vance coughed diffidently.

"So you're going to take him into custody on suspicion—eh, Sergeant? Or, perhaps, as a material witness."

"I don't care what you call it, Mr. Vance. He's going to sit around where he can't get out, doing some heavy thinking, till we get Doremus' report... You better put the bracelets on him, Emery, till we get to the corner and call the wagon."

Heath and Emery were just leading the petrified Burns to the door, when Gracie Allen came dashing back into the room, wriggling free from her mother's restraining hold.

"Oh, George, George! What's the matter? Where are they taking you? I had a feeling—like when I get psychic…"

Vance stepped to her and put both his hands on her shoulders.

"My dear child," he said in a consoling voice, "please believe me when I tell you there is nothing for you to worry about. Don't make it any harder for Mr. Burns… Won't you trust me?"

Her head dropped, and she turned to her mother. The two officers, with Burns between them, had already left the room; and, as Vance turned and reopened the door, Mrs. Allen's gentle voice spoke again.

"Thank you, sir. I am sure Gracie trusts you—just as I do."

The girl's head was on her mother's shoulder.

"Oh, Mom," she sniffled. "I don't *really* care about George not dressing as snappy as Mr. Puttle."

CHAPTER TEN

An Unexpected Visitor
(Sunday, May 19; noon.)

WHEN THE PATROL WAGON arrived and the unhappy Burns was stepping into it, Vance smiled at him encouragingly.

"Cheerio," he said; and then stood watching the wagon as it drove off. As soon as it was out of sight he summoned a taxicab and went at once to the District Attorney's apartment.

"Really, Markham," he began, "Sergeant Heath is far too logical. Ordin'rily I'd welcome such admirable mentation; but in this case I must sue for your intervention."

He then gave Markham a concise summary of all the events that had taken place since we left his apartment the night before; the trip to the mortuary and the promise to Mrs. Allen; Heath's appropriation of the cigarette case and his all-night search for Burns; the interview with the befuddled young

man when he was found; and, finally, Heath's decision to hold
Burns until Doremus reported.

Markham listened attentively, but without enthusiasm.

"I think, all in all, Heath has done a fairly intelligent
piece of work. I can't see just where, or why, you want me to
intervene."

"Burns is innocent," asserted Vance. "And I'm obdurate
in my belief. *Ergo*, I want you to call the police station and tell
Heath to release him. In fact, Markham, I insist upon it. But I
want the Sergeant to bring the chappie up here first—if that's
convenient for you. Y' see, I want him to understand clearly
that one condition of his freedom is absolute silence, for the
present, on the matter of the johnnie in the morgue. That was
our promise to Mrs. Allen, and Burns must cooperate with us
when he is released... Please hasten, old dear."

"You know this Burns?" asked Markham.

"I've seen him but twice. But I have my whimsies, don't
y' know."

"As good a euphemism as any for your present unbalanced
state of mind!... Just why do you want this fellow released?"

"I'm enraptured with the wood-nymph," smiled Vance.

Markham drew his lips together in annoyance.

"If I didn't know you, I'd say—"

"Tut, tut!... Call Heath—there's a good fellow."

Markham rose resignedly: he had known Vance too
long not to perceive the seriousness so often hid beneath his
bantering. Then he went toward the telephone.

"This is *your* case," he said, "—if it *is* a case—and you can
handle it any way you see fit. I have my own troubles."

The Sergeant had just reached the station when Markham
called and gave orders in accord with Vance's request.

Fifteen minutes later Heath escorted Burns into the
District Attorney's library. Vance carefully outlined the circumstances to Burns, and exacted from him a definite promise to
make no mention of Philip Allen's death to anyone, impressing
upon him the situation with regard to Gracie Allen herself.

George Burns, with unmistakable sincerity, readily enough agreed to the restriction; and the Sergeant informed him he was free to go.

When we were alone, however, Heath began to fume.

"After all my work last night!" he complained bitterly. "Runnin' down that cigarette case; losing my sleep and doing plenty of fancy work this morning; tying that guy in bow-knots and getting him just where I wanted him!... And it was all your idea, Mr. Vance. And now I find you something definite, and what do you do? You have the baby turned loose!"

He chewed viciously on his cigar.

"But if you think I'm not going to keep that guy covered, you ain't so smart, Mr. Vance. I sent Tracy up here ahead of me, and he's going to tail Burns from the minute he steps out of this building."

"I rather expected you would do just that, don't y' know." Vance shrugged pleasantly. "But please, Sergeant, don't get an erroneous impression from my whim to free the young perfume mixer. I shall put all my energy into unravelin' the present tangle. And I shall await the Medical Examiner's report all atwitter... By the by, in the midst of your energetic activities, did you learn anything about the autopsy?"

"Sure I did," said Heath. "I called up Doc Doremus just before I left the station. He gave me hell, as usual, but he said he'd get busy right after lunch, and that he'd have the report tonight."

"Most gratifyin'," sighed Vance. "I salute you, Sergeant, and beg forgiveness for upsettin' your admirable but useless plan to deprive Mr. Burns of his liberty. I do hope, y' know, it won't distract your mind from safeguardin' Mr. Markham from the shadow of Pellinzi."

"Nothin's going to distract me from worrying about the Buzzard and Mr. Markham," Heath asserted. "Don't you worry! That office is being watched day and night; and there's husky lads on hand to pluck that bird proper if he shows up."

The Sergeant left us a few minutes later, and we accepted Markham's invitation to remain for lunch.

It was almost three o'clock when Vance and I returned to his apartment. Currie met us at the door, looking highly perturbed.

"I'm horribly upset, sir," he said *sotto voce*. "There's a most incredible young person here waiting to see you. I tried most firmly to send her away, sir; but I couldn't seem to make her understand. She was most determined and—and hoydenish, sir." He took a quick backward glance. "I've been watching her very carefully, and I'm sure she has touched nothing. I do hope, sir—"

"You're forgiven, Currie." Vance broke into the distracted old man's apologies, and, handing him his hat and stick, went directly into the library.

Gracie Allen was sitting in Vance's large lounge chair, engulfed in the enormous tufted upholstery. When she leaped up to greet Vance it was without her former exuberance.

"Hello, Mr. Vance," she said solemnly. "I bet you didn't expect to see me. And I bet you don't know where I got your address. And the grouchy old man who met me at the door didn't expect to see me either. But I didn't tell you how I got your address. I got it the same way I got your name—*right on your card.* Though I really don't feel like going down and getting that new dress tomorrow. Maybe I won't go. That is, maybe I'll wait till I know that nothing's happened to George..."

"I'm very glad you were so clever as to find my address." Vance's tone was subdued. "And I'm delighted you're still using the citron scent."

"Oh, yes!" She looked at him gratefully. "You know, I didn't like it so much at first, but now—somehow—I just love it! Isn't that funny? But I believe in people changing their minds. Just suppose—"

"Yes," nodded Vance, with a faint smile. "Consistency is the hobgoblin—"

"But I don't believe in hobgoblins—that is, I haven't since I was a little girl."

"No, of course not."

"And when I found out you lived so close to me, I thought that was awfully convenient, because I just *had* to ask you a lot of important questions." She looked up at Vance as if to see how he would react to this announcement. "And oh, I discovered something else about you! You have five letters in your name— just like me and George. It's Fate, isn't it? If you had six letters maybe I wouldn't have come. But now I know everything is going to come out all right, isn't it?"

"Yes, my dear," nodded Vance. "I'm sure it will."

She released her breath suddenly, as if some controversial point had successfully been disposed of.

"And now I want you to tell me exactly why those policemen took George away. I'm really frightfully worried and upset, although George phoned me he was all right."

Vance sat down facing the girl.

"You really need not be concerned about Mr. Burns," he began. "The men who took him away this morning foolishly thought there were some suspicious circumst'nces connected with him. But everything will be cleared up in a day or two. Please trust me."

There was complete confidence in her frank gaze.

"But it must have been something very serious that made those men come to my house this morning and upset George so terribly."

"But," explained Vance, "they only *thought* it was serious. The truth is, my dear, a man was found dead last night at the *Domdaniel*, and—"

"But what could George have to do with *that*, Mr. Vance?"

"Really, y' know, I'm certain he has nothing to do with it."

"Then why did the men act so funny about the cigarette case I gave George? How did *they* get it, anyhow?"

Vance hesitated several moments; then he apparently reached a decision as to how far he should enlighten the girl.

"As a matter of fact," he explained patiently, "Mr. Burns' cigarette case was found in the pocket of the man who died."

"Oh! But George wouldn't give away anything *I* bought for him."

"As I say, I think it was all a great mistake."

The girl looked at Vance long and searchingly.

"But suppose, Mr. Vance—suppose this man didn't just die. Suppose he was—well—suppose he was killed, like you said you killed that bad man in Riverdale yesterday. And suppose George's cigarette case was found in his pocket. And suppose—oh, *lots* of things like that. I've read in the papers how policemen sometimes think that somebody is killed by innocent people, and how—" She stopped abruptly and put her hands to her mouth in horror.

Vance leaned over and put his hand on her arm.

"Please, please, my dear child!" he said. "You're beginning to believe in hobgoblins again. And you mustn't. They're such ridiculous little imps; and they don't really exist. Nothing is going to happen to Mr. Burns."

"But it might!" Her fears were but slightly allayed. "Can't you see, it *might*! And you've got to be an awfully, *awfully* good detective if anything like that should happen."

A frightened, pleading look was in her eyes.

"I was terribly worried this morning after George had gone. And do you know what I did? I went uptown and talked with Delpha. I always go to Delpha when I have any troubles—and sometimes even when I haven't any. And she always says she's glad to see me, because she likes to have me around. I guess it's because I'm so psychic. And having psychic people around makes it easy for you to concentrate, doesn't it?... She's got the *queerest* place, Delpha has. It makes you feel spooky at first. She's got long black curtains hanging all around, and you can't see any windows. And there's only one door; and when the black drapes are pulled across it, you just feel as though you were somewhere far away with only Delpha and the spirits that tell her things."

She looked about her and shook herself slightly.

"And then, Delpha has great big pictures of hands on the curtains, with lots of lines on them. And funny signs, too—

Delpha calls them symbols. And there's a big glass ball on a table, and a little one. And maps of the stars, with funny words around them which mean something in case you're a crab or a fish or a goat, or things like that."

"And what did Delpha tell you?" Vance asked with kindly interest.

"Oh! I didn't tell you, did I?" The girl's face brightened. "She was *very* mystical, and she seemed *terribly* surprised when I told her about George. She asked me the *funniest* questions: all about the men that came to the house, and about the cigarette case—you know, like she was trying to draw me out. I guess she was trying to read my mind because it was vibrating. And Delpha always says it's a great help to her when anybody is in tune. Anyhow, she said that nothing was going to happen to George—just like you say, Mr. Vance. Only, she said *I* must help him..."

She looked at Vance eagerly.

"You'll let me help you get George out of trouble, won't you? Mother said you told her you were going to do everything you could. I *know* I can be a sort of detective, if you tell me how. You see, I've simply *got* to help George."

Vance, puzzled and disturbed by the girl's genuine appeal, rose thoughtfully and walked to the window. Finally he returned to his chair and sat down again.

"So you want to be a detective!" he said cheerfully. "I think that's an excellent idea. And I'm going to give you all the help I can. We'll work together; you shall be my assistant, so to speak. But you must keep very busy at it. And you mustn't let anyone suspect that you're doing detective work—that's the first rule."

"Oh, that's *wonderful*, Mr. Vance! Just like in a story." The girl's spirits immediately rose. "But now tell me what I must do to be a detective."

"Very well," began Vance. "Let me see... First, of course, you must make note of anything that will be helpful. Footprints in suspicious places are a good starting-point. If people walk on soft earth, they naturally leave their tracks; and then, by measuring these tracks you can tell what size shoes they were wearing..."

"But suppose they were wearing another size shoe, just to fool us?"

Vance smiled admiringly.

"That, my child," he said, "is a very wise observation. People have been known to do that very thing. However, I do not think we need be concerned with that question just yet... To go on, you should always look at desk-blotters for clues. Blotted writing can generally be read by holding it up to a mirror."

He demonstrated this point for her, and she was as fascinated as a child watching a magician.

"And then, y' know, cigarettes are very important. Should you find the butt of a cigarette, you might be able to tell who had smoked it. You would start by looking for a person who smoked that brand. And sometimes the tip of the cigarette will give the smoker away. If there is rouge on it, then you know it was smoked by a lady who used lipstick."

"Oh!" The girl suddenly looked crestfallen. "Maybe if I had looked carefully at the cigarette that burned my dress yesterday, I might have been able to tell who threw it."

"Possibly," Vance returned gayly. "But there are many other ways of verifying your suspicions about people. For instance, if someone had gone to commit a crime in a house where there was a watch-dog, and you knew that the dog had not barked at him, then you could conclude that the intruder was a friend of the dog. Dogs, y' know, do not bark at a friend."

"But suppose," the girl interposed, "the people kept a cat instead of a dog. Or maybe a canary. What do you do then?"

Vance could not help smiling.

"In that case, you'd have to look for other things to identify the culprit..."

"That's where the footprints would come in handy, isn't it?... But lots of people wear the same size shoes. My shoes fit mother perfectly. And, what's more, her shoes fit me."

"There are still other ways—"

"I know one!" she broke in triumphantly. "What about perfume? For instance, if we found a lady's handbag, and it smelled like *Frangipanni*, then we'd look for a lady who used *Frangipanni*—not one who used *Gardenia*... But *I* wouldn't be very good at that. Would *you*? I'm always getting odors mixed up. It makes George just furious. But *he* would be simply *wonderful* at smelling. He can tell any kind of perfume right away, and what it comes from, too, and all about it—even when I don't smell anything at all. He just has a sort of gift—like when he smelled his cigarette case this morning... But please go on, Mr. Vance."

Vance did go on, for more than half an hour, carefully impressing upon her the things he knew would interest her. There was no possible doubt of his sympathetic understanding when, as the girl was about to go, he rang for Currie and gave him explicit instructions.

"This young lady, Currie," he said, "is to be received whenever she calls here. If I am out and she should care to wait, you are to make her welcome and comfortable."

When Miss Allen had gone, Vance said to me:

"The feeling of having something to lean on, as it were, will do the child a world of good at present. She's really most unhappy, and not a little frightened. Her imagined new occupation should prove a much-needed tempor'ry tonic... Y' know, Van, I have a suspicion I'm growing a bit sentimental as the years go by. Mellowin' with age—same like the grapes of France."

And he sipped his brandy slowly.

CHAPTER ELEVEN

Folklore and Poisons
(*Sunday, May 19; 9 p.m.*)

M ARKHAM TELEPHONED VANCE at nine o'clock that evening. Vance listened attentively for several minutes, a puzzled frown deepening on his face. Finally he hung up the receiver and turned to me.

"We're going down to Markham's. Doremus is there. I don't like it—I don't at all like it, Van. Doremus called him a little while ago full of news and mystery. Didn't know where Heath was, and wanted to see Markham first, anyway. Markham must have unearthed the disgruntled Sergeant, and now wants me to come down as well. Only some cataclysmic upheaval would get the peppery Doremus sufficiently excited to seek the District Attorney out in person, instead of merely turning in his official report. Very mystifyin'."

Fifteen or twenty minutes later a cab let us out in front of Markham's home. A gruff call halted us just as we were entering the building, and Sergeant Heath came bustling down the street.

"I just got the D. A.'s message at home, and beat it right over," panted Heath. "Funny business, if you ask me, Mr. Vance."

The butler was holding the door ajar for us, and we followed him into the library, where the District Attorney and Doctor Emanuel Doremus were awaiting us.

The doctor squinted malevolently at Heath.

"It *would* be one of *your* cases," he blustered, shaking an accusing finger at the Sergeant. "Why can't you ever dig up a nice, neat, easy murder, instead of these fancy affairs?" Then he nodded greetings to Vance with a weak attempt at cheeriness.

Doremus was a small, fiery man who gave the impression of a crabbed stockbroker rather than of a highly efficient scientific man.

"I'm getting sick of these trick murders of yours," he went on to the Sergeant. "Furthermore, I haven't had any food since noon. Can't eat properly even on a Sunday. You and your crazy corpses!"

The Sergeant grinned and said nothing. He knew Doremus of old, and had long since come to accept his eccentric and sometimes querulous manner.

"No, doctor," put in Vance placatingly; "the unhappy Sergeant is merely an innocent onlooker... What seems to be the difficulty?"

"You're in on this too, eh?" Doremus retorted. "I might have known! Say, don't you like to see people shot or stabbed, pretty and clean, instead of being poisoned so I've got to work all the time?"

"Poisoned?" asked Vance curiously. "Who's been poisoned?

"The stiff I'm talking about," shouted Doremus; "the fellow Heath handed me. I forget his name."

"Philip Allen," supplied the Sergeant.

"All right, all right. He'd be just as dead with any other name. And what makes me sore is I don't know any more about what killed him than if he was a dead Zulu in Isipingo."

"You spoke of poison, doctor," prompted Vance calmly.

"I did," snapped Doremus. "But *you* tell me what kind of poison. It doesn't check with any books of mine on toxicology."

"Really, y' know, that doesn't sound exactly scientific," smiled Vance. "Hope we're not travelin' back to mysticism."

"Oh, it's scientific enough," Doremus pursued. "The poison—whatever it is—was undoubtedly absorbed through the derma or the mucous membrane. It might have been lots of things. But I couldn't get any straight-cut reaction from the regulation tests. It might have been a combination of some kind." He grunted. "I'll find it, all right. Not tonight, though. It may take a day or so. It's the damnedest thing I've ever been up against."

"I can readily believe that," said Vance, "or you wouldn't be here tonight."

"Maybe I shouldn't be. But this pest"—he indicated Heath—"kept yelling about the case being so important, and that it might have something to do with Mr. Markham. Sounded like a hoax; but I thought it best to tell him I couldn't add up the figures tonight. Let *him* worry. *I'm* hungry."

"What have I to do with this, Sergeant?" Markham's tone carried a biting reprimand.

"Wasn't it in Mirche's office, Chief?" parried Heath aggressively. "And that's where I been looking for trouble for you... And Hennessey watching, and—and everything," he ended lamely, as Vance cut him short with a wave of the hand.

"We appreciate your trouble and your courtesy, doctor," Vance said. "You're quite sure the fellow couldn't have died a natural death?"

"Not unless medical science has gone completely bughouse," Doremus returned emphatically. "This fellow was poisoned—that much I know. I don't wonder young Mendel threw up his hands. Not only was it poison, but it was a quick, powerful poison that could have taken effect at once. But it didn't act exactly like anything I'm familiar with."

"But, doctor," persisted Vance, "You must have some idea."

"Huh! I've got plenty of ideas. That's my difficulty: too damn many ideas."

"For instance?"

"Well, there's our old friend, potassium cyanide. There's plenty of indications pointing to hydrocyanic acid. I'd say he got a few sniffs of cyanide gas and passed out. The bulging eyes and the color of the skin might mean cyanide—and they might also mean something else again. And I did get a bit of the odor in the lungs and gastric mucosa. But nothing from the mouth, or when I opened the cranial cavity. But that doesn't mean anything either, especially as a lot of other things showed up that didn't spell prussic acid backwards or forwards, or two ways from the middle."

"I believe Doctor Mendel spoke of some burns—probably just a local reaction—on the lips and in the throat. What of them?"

"*You* tell me." Doremus seemed annoyed with the world in general. "My whiff of the lungs indicated a probable inhalation of something, as I've already said."

"Might it have been nitrobenzene?" suggested Vance.

"I wouldn't know—I'm just a medical man."

"Come, come, doctor," Vance said good-naturedly. "I'm merely trying to steer you clear of ancient toxic lore."

Doremus sat up with a jerk and grinned apologetically.

"I don't blame you, Mr. Vance. I'm hot and annoyed. Maybe I do sound as if I was messing around with ancient Egyptians, and mandragora, and viper venoms, and secret Gypsy potions, and witches' ointments with their henbane, and Borgia poisons, and Perugia water, and *aqua* Tofana—"

"Did you say Tofana, doc?" interrupted Heath. "That's the name of that fortune-telling Delpha, Mr. Vance. And I don't put poison beyond her and her husband."

THE GRACIE ALLEN MURDER CASE 89

"No, no, Sergeant," Vance corrected him. "The Tofana the doctor mentioned died in Sicily in the seventeenth century. And she wasn't a fortune-teller. Far from it. She devoted her talents to mixing a liquid which has since come to be known by her name. *Aqua* Tofana was a deadly poison; and this woman plied her poisoning trade on such a wholesale scale that the name of her concoction has never been forgot. Though her mixture was probably nothing but a strong solution of arsenic, there's still a lot of mystery attaching to it. That's the lady, dead for centuries, to whom Doctor Doremus was referring."

"I still say Rosa Tofana ain't beyond the same kind of tricks," insisted Heath doggedly.

"You seem astonishingly full of hatreds and suspicions, Sergeant."

"In my business I gotta be," Heath mumbled.

Vance turned back to Doremus.

"Forgive us for interrupting, doctor. We all seem to have become embittered by the present case... But what about poisons isolated from flowers? These would be difficult to trace, wouldn't they?"

"No! They're easy enough, put they'd take time. And I know 'em all. You mean, I take it, colchicine from meadow saffron, helleborin from the Christmas rose, narcissine from the daffodil, convallarin from the lily of the valley—things like that. But I assure you it wasn't anything as mild as these that did this fellow in... Or maybe—" He cocked his eye in a leer at Vance. "Now it's *you* that's talking about the so-called poisoned posies of medieval romance. Humph! Modern science laughs at 'em."

"No—oh, no. I haven't gone afield as far as that," laughed Vance. "I was merely thinking of the lavender peddler in London, who passed out when he sniffed the oil of mirbane he'd put on his flowers to enhance their aroma."

"There's nothing to that." Doremus shook his head scornfully. "I'm only saying that I don't know just now what it was this Allen man inhaled... But give me time—give me time. I'll find out tomorrow. And, what's more, it won't be as crazy as it sounds now."

"Could you say when he died, doc?" asked Heath.

Doremus glared at the Sergeant.

"How would *I* know? I'm no necromancer. I didn't even see the body till this afternoon." His anger abated at sight of Heath's discomfiture. "I talked with Doctor Mendel, but he wouldn't venture a guess. Said there was no *rigor mortis* when he first saw the body. But you can't time stiffening of the muscles with a stop-watch. The onset is highly variable—lot of different factors operating. From what I've been able to learn, the fellow could have died within a couple of hours before he was found, or he could have died as long as ten hours before... *I* don't know; *Mendel* don't know; *you* don't know..."

When Doremus had sputtered a while longer, he left us with a breezy wave of the hand.

"Well, Vance," said the District Attorney, "how are you going to fit that preposterous situation into your story?"

Vance shook his head pensively.

"I don't know, Markham. But rest assured it fits somewhere, and I'm still haunted by the various converging factors of my tale... And, Sergeant, that was a curious interpolation of yours about the Tofanas. Y' know, your friend Rosa is strangely interested in the deceased gentleman..."

He rose and walked back and forth several times.

"I'm not admitting defeat yet, Markham. There are too many questions in my mind crying out for answers. How, for instance, did the chap get into Mirche's office again after Hennessey saw him at six o'clock?"

"Hennessey musta been lookin' the other way," said Heath stolidly.

"That's not likely, Sergeant. Something very peculiar there."

He smoked for a while in silence.

"I wish I could see the plans for the remodeling of that old house when Mirche took it over for his café. There might be something suggestive about them. An odd desire, I'll admit. But I could bear to look at them."

"I don't see how those plans would do you any good," said Heath. "But if you really want 'em, I can get 'em for you easy. Doyle and Schuster did the job, and I've had dealings with their chief draughtsman before."

"That sounds hopeful, Sergeant. When could you get the blueprints for me?"

"Before you're up in the morning, sir," returned the other confidently. "Say around ten o'clock."

Markham looked amused.

"Why not get the blueprints for a couple of mare's-nests, too, while you're about it, Vance?—The sensible thing to do, it seems to me, would be to wait till you get Doremus' final report."

"You're quite right," Vance reluctantly conceded. "But my instincts don't run to so many coincidences. I crave simplicity. Besides, I have an appealin' young lady to consider."

"I assure you," said Markham unsympathetically, "after you've scanned the blueprints tomorrow, you'll have ample time to consider your young lady."

"No—no, Markham." Vance spoke soberly. "It is not a subject for levity…"

Then he told in detail of Gracie Allen's pathetic visit to him that afternoon—her appeal for help, her concern for Burns, and his own compassionate suggestions to keep her mind occupied.

"Both the Sergeant and I," he concluded, "have made a promise to her mother, and, after the girl's impromptu visit today, I want to impress upon both of you that we must be considerate whenever the girl chooses to intrude on us."

"I deem it a pleasure, not to say a rarity, to commend your sentimental punctilio," Markham said. "But I myself shall probably not be called upon to assist in the charitable deception. The brunt of the situation, it seems to me, will fall upon you and the Sergeant."

"It's all right with me, Chief," said Heath. "That Mrs. Allen is a mighty sweet little woman. And the girl is plenty cute."

Vance smiled gratefully.

"You'll have to be rather careful, Sergeant. The best way to meet the situation is to show no outward sympathy. That might make the girl suspicious. We should simply act at all times as if we knew no more about her brother's death than she does herself. An actor, Sergeant! Could you be an actor?"

"Sure I'll be an actor!" Heath voiced his decision with ready sincerity. "But I ain't so hard-boiled yet that I'm gonna promise not to sometimes get a lump in my gullet..."

He seemed a little ashamed of his unbecoming outburst of sentiment.

"Hell!" he added quickly. "I'll even be one of those damn matinée idols."

CHAPTER TWELVE

A Strange Discovery
(Monday. May 20; 9 a.m.)

VANCE HAD BEEN reluctant Sunday evening to leave Markham's apartment, and had remained late. But he was up earlier than usual the following morning. By half-past eight he was completely dressed and had drunk his coffee. Shortly after nine, Sergeant Heath arrived, striding into the library in jaunty triumph.

"Here you are, Mr. Vance," he announced, placing a long cardboard tube on the desk. "If all my jobs were as easy as getting these blueprints for you, I'd never die from overwork."

"My word, such efficiency!"

Vance drew the plans from their holder and spread them on the desk. He scrutinized them all, inspecting the sheet for each floor in turn. He gave more time, however, to the ground-floor plan which included the actual café room, the entrance hall and the check-rooms, the kitchen quarters, and the office. The Sergeant watched him with expectant amusement.

"Quite conventional," Vance murmured, tapping the sheets with his finger. "An excellent bit of planning. Intelligently done. No more, no less. Sad...sad."

At this moment Gracie Allen unexpectedly arrived. She preceded Currie into the room, making his announcement superfluous.

"Oh, I just *had* to come and see you, Mr. Vance! Somehow I don't seem to be getting anywhere—and I worked *so* hard. Honest, I did!"

"But my word! young lady,"—Vance spoke pleasantly— "why aren't you at the factory this morning?"

"I just couldn't go there," she returned. "Not for a while, anyhow. I've got so *much* on my mind—that is, terribly important things. And I'm sure Mr. Doolson won't mind... George didn't go to the factory today, either. He phoned me last night and said he couldn't possibly do *anything*. He's so upset."

"Well, perhaps after all, Miss Allen, a few days' rest—"

"Oh, I'm not resting." She appeared hurt. "I'm *frightfully* busy every minute. You yourself said I have to keep busy. Remember?" She caught sight of Heath, and a frightened look came into her large eyes as she recognized him.

Vance eased the situation by casually introducing the Sergeant.

"He is working with us, too," he added. "You can trust the Sergeant. I explained his error to him yesterday, and now he's on our side... Furthermore," Vance went on cheerfully, "he has five letters in his name."

"Oh!" Her fears were somewhat allayed by this information, though she looked dubiously at Heath again before she broke into a faint smile. Then she pointed to the desk. "What are all those blue papers, Mr. Vance?—they weren't there yesterday. Maybe they're a clue, or something. Are they?"

"No, I'm afraid not. They're just plans of the *Domdaniel* where you were Saturday night..."

"Oh, may I look?"

"Certainly," Vance replied, and bent over the desk with her. "See, this is the big dining room, and the entrance door from the hall; and over here is the kitchen, and the side door; and right along here is the driveway that goes under the arch; and right in this corner is the office, with the door opening on the terrace; and—"

"Wait a minute," she interrupted. "That's not *really* an office."

She bent closer over the chart and traced corridors and directions with her finger, calling them off as she did so. She ended by following the outline of the small room. Then she looked up.

"Why, that's Dixie Del Marr's *private* room. She told me so herself... Don't you think she's just *beautiful*, Mr. Vance? And she can sing so lovely, too. I wish I could sing like her. You know, classical songs."

"I'm sure your singing is much prettier," Vance told her gallantly. "But I think you're mistaken about that room being Miss Del Marr's. Really, y' know, it's Mr. Mirche's office—isn't it, Sergeant?"

"I'll say it is!"

Gracie Allen bent still lower over the papers.

"Oh, but it *is* the room I was in," she asserted conclusively. "I'll show you—that window looks right out on the driveway; and here's the street, through those tiny windows. It even says '50th Street' right on the picture. Why, it's *got* to be Miss Del Marr's room. And you can't have two rooms in the same place, can you—even in a picture?"

"No, not very well—"

"And aren't the walls all done in mauve? And aren't there three or four big leather chairs along this wall? And isn't there a big dead fish on a board, hanging up here?" She pointed out the locations as she spoke. "And isn't there a funny little glass chandelier hanging—Oh, where's the ceiling, Mr. Vance? I don't see any ceiling on this picture."

Heath had become highly interested in the girl's inventory.

"Sure," he said. "The walls are a sort of light purple; and Mirche says he caught that fish down in Florida. She's dead right, Mr. Vance... But see here, Miss, when were you ever in that room?"

"Why, I was in it just last Saturday night."

"What!" bellowed Heath.

The girl was startled.

"Did I say something wrong? I didn't *mean* to go in there."

Vance spoke now.

"What time during the evening did you go in there, Miss Allen?"

"Why, *you* know, Mr. Vance. When I went to look for Philip, at ten o'clock... But I didn't see Philip. He wasn't around. And he didn't come home yesterday, either. I guess he's gone on a vacation somewhere. And he *promised* he wouldn't quit his job."

Vance diverted the girl's aimless chatter.

"Let's not talk about Philip now. Just tell me how you happened to go out on the terrace looking for your brother, when you really wanted to go to the rear of the café."

"I didn't go out on the terrace." She shook her head emphatically. "What would I want to go on the terrace for, anyhow? I'd have caught cold in that thin dress I was wearing. Don't you think that was an *awfully* pretty dress, Mr. Vance? Mother made that too."

"Yes, you looked very charming in it... But you must have forgot, for the only way to get into that room is from the terrace."

"Oh, but I went in the *other* way—through the door at the back." She pointed to the wall directly opposite the street door of Mirche's office; then her eyes opened wide as she scrutinized the blueprint. "There's something *awfully* funny here, Mr. Vance. Whoever made this picture wasn't very careful."

Vance came closer to her. The Sergeant, too, moved nearer, and stood beside them with an air of curious expectancy, his cigar poised in mid-air.

"You think there should be another door shown at that spot?" Vance asked softly.

"Why, of course! Because there *is* a door right there. Otherwise, how could I have gotten in Miss Del Marr's private room? But I can't *imagine* why she keeps that fish in there. I don't think it's pretty at all."

"Don't worry about the fish. Look here at the plan a minute... Now, here's the archway through which you left the dining room—"

"Uh-huh. The one with the big carved stairway in front of it."

"And then—let's see—you must have gone this way in the hall—"

"That's right. George wanted me to stay and speak to him, but I was in a hurry. So I went right on back, until I passed another little hallway. And then I didn't know *which* way to go."

"You must have turned into that narrow passage, and walked down to this point, here." Vance brought to a stop the pencil with which he was tracing her course on the blueprint.

"That's just what I did! How do you know? Were you watching me?"

"No, my dear," Vance answered patiently. "But maybe you're a little confused. There is a door here, at the end of this narrow passage, where you say you walked down."

"Yes, I saw that door. I even opened it. But there wasn't anything there—only the driveway. That's how I knew I was lost. And then as I stood there leaning against the wall and wondering how to find Philip, this other door I was telling you about—you know, the one into Miss Del Marr's room—opened right behind me." She tittered, as at some joke she was just about to relate. "And I fell *right into the room!* It was terribly embarrassing. But I didn't spoil my dress at all. And I might have *torn* it, falling like that... I guess it was my own fault though, for not looking where I was leaning. But I didn't know there was a door there. I didn't see any door at all. Anyhow, there I was in the room. Isn't that *silly*—not seeing a door and leaning up against it, and then falling down right into a lady's room?" She laughed engagingly at the recital of her mishap.

Vance led the girl to a chair and arranged a pillow for her.

"Sit right there, my dear," he said, "and tell us all about it."

"But I *have* told you," she said, arranging herself comfortably. "It was *awfully* funny; and I was *so* embarrassed. Miss Del Marr was embarrassed too. She told me that was her private room. So, I told her I was *awfully* sorry and explained about looking for my brother—she even knew Philip. I guess that's because they both work at the same place, like me and George... And then she showed me back down the hall, and pointed out the exact way to the landing on the kitchen stairs. She was awfully nice. Well, I waited a long time, but Philip didn't show up. So I went back to Mr. Puttle. I knew how to find my way back, all right... And now, Mr. Vance, I want to ask you some more questions about what you said yesterday—"

"I'd love to answer them, Miss Allen," Vance said; "but I really haven't any time this morning. Maybe later—this afternoon. You won't mind, will you?"

"Oh, no." The girl jumped up quickly. "I've got something very important to do, too. And maybe George will come up for a while." She shook Vance's hand, nodded suspiciously to Heath, and in a moment she was gone.

"*Holy suffering sauerkraut!*" exploded Heath, almost before the door closed on Miss Allen. "Didn't I tell you that Mirche was a crafty customer? So he's got a secret door! The dizzy doll didn't see it—sure she didn't! Somebody musta got careless—her leanin' up against a invisible door and goin' *plop*—right into the room where her brother was killed! That's somethin'!"

Vance smiled grimly.

"But, after all, Sergeant, there's no law against a man having a secret door to his own office. And that, undoubtedly, is our answer to the question of how the dead fellow got in there without being seen by Hennessey. But someone must have been in there with him. Not Mirche: he was at my table between ten and eleven. And certainly no dead man was there at ten."

"But don't you think Mr. Vance—"

"Spare me, Sergeant!" Vance was pacing the floor.

"I'd like to go up to the *Domdaniel* and smash that fake door in!" Heath asserted violently.

"No—oh, no," counseled Vance. "You mustn't be impetuous. Silkiness. Let that be your watchword for the nonce."

"Still and all," said the determined Heath, "if this *Domdaniel*'s the headquarters for a crooked ring of some kind, like I've always suspected, nothing'd give me more pleasure than smashing the whole place—and Mirche along with it."

"Your nature's too vehement, Sergeant," Vance rebuked him. "One doesn't go about shattering people's offices without proof of their guilt."

"I'm just sayin' what I'd *like* to do."

"And another thing, Sergeant: Mirche would be merely one weak link in your imagin'ry criminal chain. As I said, he's far from being a leader of men."

"He looks like a pretty slick article to me," Heath remonstrated meekly. "Anyhow, that 'Owl' Owen you was worrying about would fill the bill."

"Quite—quite," mused Vance. "But he was merely a fellow diner when I saw him. Very correct and unobtrusive. Though I admit I didn't relish his being there that night, with so many other queer things all coming together and signifying nothing." He made an ambiguous gesture. "I think we may forget him for the present, and concentrate on ascertaining who killed the poor chap."

"Yeah? How? By checkin' up a little closer on Mirche?"

"Precisely, Sergeant. And I sha'n't overlook Dixie Del Marr either. Not after that amazing information about the door into *her* private room."

"And just how do you intend doing it, Mr. Vance?"

"Quite openly, Sergeant. I shall drop in for a chat... Where, by the by, does brother Mirche reside?"

"That's easy," Heath told him. "Upstairs at the *Domdaniel*."

"I thought as much… And could you answer with equal ease if I asked you the domicile of Miss Del Marr?"

"Sure." Heath grunted. "I wouldn't have lasted this long on the homicide squad, if I didn't know where the people live that I think are crooked and mixed up in dirty business. You'll find her at the Antler Hotel, on 53rd Street."

"You're a fund of information, Sergeant," Vance complimented him.

"When do you intend to see 'em, sir?… And then what?"

"I'll try to commune with Mirche and Miss Del Marr this very morning. After that, I'll endeavor to lure Mr. Markham to lunch. Then I should be charmed to meet you here again at three this afternoon."

"It's still your case, Mr. Vance," mumbled Heath. "I'm not goin' to tell you how to handle it." He remained another half-hour before taking his departure.

Then Vance telephoned to Markham, after which he sat down and lighted a cigarette, with more than ordinary deliberation.

"Still another amazin' facet in the gem, Van," he said. "Markham was on the point of calling me when I was put through to his office. Mr. Doolson—he of the In-O-Scent Corporation—had just come and gone. Markham promised he'd pour forth the story when I see him later—he seemed inordin'tely amused. We're to be at his office round one o'clock. I told him if we weren't there by two, to send a posse of trusty stalwarts to our rescue at the *Domdaniel*."

CHAPTER THIRTEEN

News of an Owl
(Monday, May 20; 11 a.m.)

At ELEVEN O'CLOCK Vance went to the *Domdaniel*.
He had no difficulty about seeing Mirche. After a delay of
only five minutes, Mirche came into the reception hall where
we were waiting. He greeted Vance effusively, though he
gave me the impression that he was acting out a rehearsed
part.

"To what am I indebted for this unexpected visit, sir?" he
asked smoothly.

"I merely wanted a chat with you anent the poor fellow
who was found dead here Saturday night." Vance spoke with a
casual pleasantness.

"Oh, yes." If Mirche was surprised, he disguised the fact
successfully. "Of course, if it's about his family, we will be very
glad to see what can be done... Naturally, I should like to avoid

any scandal—the public is sensitive about such matters. A most unfortunate incident. But suppose we go into my office."

He led the way along the terrace, and opening the door, stood aside to let us precede him. Vance seated himself in one of the large leather chairs, and Mirche sat down half facing him.

"The police have naturally been asking a great many questions about the affair," Mirche began. "But I was hoping the whole thing had been settled by now."

"These things are most distressin', I know," said Vance. "But there are one or two points about the situation that rather interest me."

"I'm greatly surprised that you should be interested, Mr. Vance." Mirche was cool and suave. "After all, the man was only a dishwasher here. I had dismissed him just before the dinner hour. A question of pay—he didn't think he was getting enough. I don't see why he should have come back, unless he thought better of the matter and wished to be reinstated. Most unfortunate he should die in my office. But he didn't seem to be a particularly robust fellow, and I suppose one can never tell when the heart will give out... By the way, Mr. Vance, have they found out just what did cause his death?"

"No, I don't believe so," answered Vance noncommittally. "However, that isn't the point that interests me at the moment. The fact is, Mr. Mirche, there was an officer in the street outside Saturday night, and he insists he didn't see this dishwasher of yours enter the office here, after he was last seen coming out of it at about six o'clock."

"Probably didn't notice him," said Mirche indifferently.

"No—oh, no. The officer—who, by the by, knew young Allen—is quite positive the man did not enter your office from the balcony all evening."

Mirche looked up and spread his hands.

"I must still insist, Mr. Vance—"

"Is it possible the fellow could have come in here some other way?" Vance paused momentarily and looked about him.

"He might, don't y' know, have come through that little door in the wall at the rear."

Mirche did not speak for a moment. He stared shrewdly at Vance, and the muscles in his body seemed to tighten. If I have ever seen a living picture of a man thinking rapidly, Mirche was that picture.

Suddenly the man let out a short laugh.

"And I thought I had guarded my little secret so well!... That door is a device of mine—purely for my own convenience, you understand." He rose and went to the rear of the office. "I'll show you how it works." He pressed a small medallion on the wainscoting, and a panel barely two feet wide swung silently into the room. Beyond was the narrow passageway in which Gracie Allen had lost her way.

Vance looked at the concealed catch on the secret door and then turned away, as if the revelation were nothing new to him.

"Quite neat," he drawled.

"A great convenience," said Mirche, closing the door. "A private entrance to my office from the café. You can see, Mr. Vance—"

"Oh, yes—quite. Useful no end when you crave a bit of privacy. I've known certain Wall-Street brokers to have just such contraptions. Can't say I blame them... But how should your dishwasher have known of this arrangement?"

Mirche stroked his chin thoughtfully.

"I'm sure I don't know. Although it's wholly possible, of course, that some of the help around here have spied on me— or perhaps run into the secret accidentally."

"Miss Del Marr's aware of it, of course?"

"Oh, yes," Mirche admitted. "She helps me here a bit at times. I see no reason for not letting her use the door when she wishes."

It was apparent that Vance was somewhat taken aback at Mirche's frankness, and he straightway turned the conversation into other channels. He put numerous questions about Allen, and then reverted to the events of Saturday night.

In the midst of one of Vance's questions the front door opened, and Miss Del Marr herself appeared in the doorway. Mirche invited her in and immediately introduced us.

"I have just been telling these gentlemen," he said quickly, "about the private entrance to this room." He forced a laugh. "Mr. Vance seemed to think there might be some mysterious connection between that and—"

Vance held up his hand, protesting pleasantly.

"I'm afraid you read hidden meanings into my words, Mr. Mirche." Then he smiled at Miss Del Marr. "You must find that door a great convenience."

"Oh, yes—especially when the weather is bad. In fact, it has proved most convenient." She spoke in a casual tone, but there was a hardness, almost a bitterness, in her expression.

Vance was scrutinizing her closely. I expected him to question her regarding Allen's death, for I knew this had been his intention. But, instead, he chatted carelessly regarding trivial things, quite unrelated to the matter which had brought him there.

Shortly before he made his adieus, he said disarmingly to Miss Del Marr: "Forgive me if I seem personal, but I cannot help admiring the scent you are wearing. I'd hazard a guess it is a blend of jonquille and rose."

If the woman was astonished at Vance's comment, she gave no indication of it.

"Yes," she replied indifferently. "It has a ridiculous name— quite unworthy of it, I think. Mr. Mirche uses the perfume, too—I am sure it was my influence." She gave the man a conventional smile; and again I detected the hardness and bitterness in her manner.

We took our leave soon thereafter, and as we walked toward Seventh Avenue, Vance was unusually serious.

"Deuced clever, our Mr. Mirche," he muttered. "Can't understand why he wasn't more concerned about the secret door. He's worried, though. Oh, quite. Very queer... No need whatever to question the Lorelei. Changed my mind about that the moment she spoke so dulcetly and looked at Mirche. *There* was hatred, Van—passionate, cruel hatred... And they both use *Kiss Me Quick*. Oh, where does that aromatic item belong?... Most puzzlin'!..."

At the District Attorney's office Markham told us about Doolson's visit that morning.

"The man is desperately concerned, Vance—and for the most incredible reason. It seems he has an exalted opinion of this young Burns' ability. Imagines his perfumery business cannot function without the fellow. Is convinced that Burns holds the key to the factory's continued success. And more of that sort of amazing twaddle."

"Not twaddle at all, Markham," Vance put in. "Doolson probably has every reason to regard Burns highly. It was Burns who concocted the formula for *In-O-Scent* and saved Doolson from bankruptcy. I understand just what the man means."

"Well, it seems, further, that the business of the concern is of a somewhat seasonal nature and that the annual peak is approaching. Doolson has invested heavily in an intensive campaign of some kind, and is in immediate need of various new popular odors. His contention is that only Burns can turn the trick."

"Both interesting and plausible. But why his visit here to your sanctum?"

"It appears Burns has chucked his job until cleared of all suspicion in the Allen affair. He's nervous and, I imagine, not a little frightened. Can't work, can't think, can't sniff—completely disorganized. And Doolson is frantic. He had a talk with the fellow this morning, and got the reasons for his obstinate refusal to return to his work. Burns told him the affair was being kept quiet temporarily, and gave no names; but explained that he was in some way concerned with it and therefore upset. Having complete faith in Burns, Doolson hastened here in despair. Probably thought my office wasn't making enough speed."

"Well?"

"He insists on offering a reward for the solution to the case, in the desperate hope of spurring me and the staff to get the matter settled at once, so his precious Burns can get back to work. Personally, I think the man is crazy."

"It could be, Markham. But don't disabuse him."

"I've already tried. But he was insistent."

"And at what figure does he estimate the immediate and carefree services of Mr. Burns?"

"Five thousand dollars!"

"Quite insane," Vance laughed.

"I agree with you. I wouldn't believe it myself if I didn't have the written and signed instructions and the certified check right here in my safe at this moment—incidentally, with an expiration clause of forty-eight hours."

After Vance had absorbed this fantastic information, he related his own activities of the morning. He told of the secret door to Mirche's office, and dwelt on the Sergeant's stubborn suspicion that the *Domdaniel* was the centre of some far-reaching criminal ring.

To this last, Markham nodded slowly and thoughtfully.

"I'm not sure," he remarked, "that the Sergeant's suspicions are unfounded. That place has always troubled me a bit, but nothing definite has ever been brought to light."

"The Sergeant mentioned Owen as a possible guiding genius," Vance said. "And the idea rather appeals to me. I'm half inclined, don't y' know, to search for the 'Owl' and see if I can ruffle his feathers... By the by, Markham, in case my impulse should overcome my discretion, what might be his given name? Really, one can't go about inquiring for a predat'ry nocturnal bird."

"As I remember, it's Dominic."

"Dominic—Dominic..." Suddenly Vance stood up, his eyes fixed before him. "*Dominic* Owen! And *Daniel* Mirche!" He held his cigarette suspended. "Now the whole thing *has* become fantasy. You're right, Markham—I'm having visions:

I'm enmeshed in an abracadabra. It's all as fantastic as the Papyrus of Ani!"

"In the name of Heaven—" began Markham.

"Doesn't it pierce your consciousness?" Then he said: "*Dominic—Daniel.* To wit, *DOMDANIEL!*"

Markham raised his eyebrows skeptically.

"Sheer coincidence, Vance. Though a neat bit of fantasy, I'll admit. As I recall my *Arabian Nights,* the original Domdaniel was under the ocean, somewhere near Tunis, and was the abode of evil spirits. Even if Mirche had ever heard of that undersea palace and *was* a partner of Owen's in the café, he'd never have had enough initiative, or courage, for that."

"Not Mirche, Markham. But Owen. He would have the subtlety and the daring and the grim humor. The idea would have been quite magnificent, don't y' know. Offering the world a key to his secret, and then chuckling to himself much like one of the evil afrits who originally inhabited that subterranean citadel of sin..."

He commiserated with Markham on the intricacies of life, and left him to draw his own conclusions.

It was not Heath who was waiting for us when we returned to Vance's apartment a little before three. It was the ubiquitous Gracie Allen; and, as usual, she greeted Vance with gay exuberance.

"You told me to come back this afternoon. Or didn't you? Anyhow, you did say something about later this afternoon, and I didn't know what time *that* was; so I thought I'd come early. I've got *lots* of clues collected—that is, I've got three or four. But I don't think they're any good. Have *you* got any clues, Mr. Vance?"

"Not yet," he said, smiling. "That is, I haven't any definite clues. But I have several ideas."

"Oh, tell me all about your ideas, Mr. Vance," she urged. "Maybe they *will* help. You never know what will come out of just thinking. Only last week I thought there'd be a thunderstorm—and there *was!*"

"Well, let me see..." And Vance, somewhat in the spirit of facetiousness, yet with a manifest benignity, told her of his surmise regarding the meaning of the word "Domdaniel." He dwelt entertainingly on the mystery and romance of the *Arabian Nights* legend of the original Domdaniel—the Syrian califs, the "roots of the ocean," the four entrances and the four thousand steps, and Maghrabi and the other magicians and sorcerers.

Heath had come in at the beginning of the story, and stood listening throughout as enthralled as was the girl. When Vance had finished Gracie Allen relaxed momentarily.

"That's simply *wonderful*, Mr. Vance. I wish I could help you find the man named Dominic. We have a big fat shipping clerk down at the factory named Dominic. But he can't be the one you mean."

"No, I'm sure he's not. This one is a small man, with very dark, piercing eyes, and a white face, and hair that's almost black."

"Oh! Maybe it was the man I saw in Miss Del Marr's room."

"What!" The Sergeant's exclamation startled the girl.

"Goodness! Did I say something wrong *again*, Mr. Heath?"

Vance reproachfully waved the Sergeant back. Then he spoke calmly to the girl.

"You mean, Miss Allen, that you saw someone besides Miss Del Marr when you fell into that room last Saturday?"

"Yes. A man *exactly* like you described."

"But why," asked Vance, "did you not tell me about him this morning?"

"Why, you didn't ask me! If you'd *asked* me I'd have told you. And anyhow, I didn't think it made any difference—about the man being there, I mean. *He* didn't have anything *at all* to do with my tumble."

"And you're sure," Vance went on, "that he looked like the man I just described to you?"

"Uh-huh, I'm sure."

"I don't suppose you had ever seen him before."

"I never saw him before in all my life. And I'd have remembered, too, if I'd ever seen him. I *always* remember faces, but I can't hardly *ever* remember names. But I did see him *afterwards*."

"Afterwards? Where was that?"

"Why, he was sitting in the dining room, right in the corner, not very far from George. I can't *imagine* how I happened to look over in that direction, because I *was* with Mr. Puttle that evening."

"Was there anyone else with the man when you saw him in the dining room?" Vance pursued.

"But I couldn't see *them*, because they had their backs to me."

"Them? Just whom do you mean?"

"Why, the two other men at the same table."

Vance inhaled deeply on his cigarette.

"Tell me, Miss Allen: what was the man doing when you saw him in Miss Del Marr's room?"

"Well, let me see. I guess he was a *very* personal friend of Miss Del Marr's because he was putting a big notebook away in one of the drawers. And he *must* have been a very personal friend of Miss Del Marr's, or he wouldn't know where the book belonged, would he? And then Miss Del Marr came over to me and put her hand on my arm, and led me out very quick. I guess she was in a hurry. But she was *awfully* nice..."

"Well, that was a very amusing experience, my dear."

Shortly after this astounding recital, Miss Allen cheerfully took leave of us, saying, with a comical air of mystery, that she had a lot of very important things to attend to. She intimated that she might even be seeing Mr. Burns.

When she had gone Vance looked across at the Sergeant as if expecting some comment.

Heath sprawled in a chair, apparently stunned.

"I got nothin' to say, Mr. Vance. I'm goin' nuts!"

"I'm a bit groggy myself," said Vance. "But now it's imperative that I see Owen. Frankly, I've been only half-hearted about communing with him, and only vaguely believed in my game of charades about Owen and Mirche. Yet Gracie Allen knew of the connection all along. Yes, now it *is* highly imperative that I tree the 'Owl.' Can you help, Sergeant?"

Heath pursed his lips.

"I don't know where the guy's staying in New York, if that's what you mean. But one of the federal boys I know might have the dope. Wait a minute..."

He went to the telephone in the hall, while Vance smoked in silent preoccupation.

"At last I got it," Heath announced as he came back into the room a half-hour later. "None of the federal boys knew Owen was in town, but one of 'em dug up the file and told me that Owen used to live at the St. Carlton during the old investigation. I took a chance and called up the hotel. He's stopping there, all right—got in Thursday..."

"Thank you, Sergeant. I'll phone you in the morning. In the meantime, discourage thought."

The Sergeant departed, and Vance immediately put a call through to Markham.

"You're breakfasting with me tomorrow," he told the District Attorney. "This evening I shall endeavor to call on the erudite Mr. Owen. I've many things to tell you, and I may have more by morning. Remember, Markham: breakfast tomorrow—it's a ukase, not a frivolous invitation..."

CHAPTER FOURTEEN

A Dying Madman
(Monday. May 20; 8 p.m.)

Aт EIGHT O'CLOCK that evening Vance went to the
St. Carlton hotel. He did not telephone from the reception
desk, but wrote the word "Unprofessionally" across one of his
personal cards and sent it to Owen. A few minutes later the
bellboy returned and led us upstairs.

Two men were standing by a window when we entered,
and Owen himself was seated limply in a low chair against the
wall, slowly turning Vance's card between his slender tapering
fingers. He looked at Vance, and tossed the card on the inlaid
tabouret beside him. Then he said in a soft, imperious voice,
"That's all tonight." The two men went out of the room immediately, and closed the door.

"Forgive me," he said with a wistful, apologetic smile.
"Man is a suspicious animal." He moved his hand in a vague

gesture: it was his invitation for us to sit down. "Yes, suspicious. But why should one care?" Owen's voice was ominously low, but it had a plaintive carrying quality, like a birdcall at dusk. "I know why you came. And I am glad to see you. Something might have intervened."

With a closer view of the man, I got the impression that grave illness hung over him. An inner lethargy marked him; his eyes were liquid; his face was almost cyanosed; his voice a monotone. He gave me the feeling of a living dead man.

"For several years," he went on, "there has been the vagrant hope that some day... Need for consciousness of kind, like-mindedness..." His voice drifted off.

"The loneliness of psychic isolation," murmured Vance. "Quite. Perhaps I was not the one."

"Nobody is the one, of course. Forgive my conceit." Owen smiled wanly and lighted a cigarette. "You think that either of us willed this meeting? Man makes no choices. His choice is his temperament. We are sucked into a vortex, and until we escape we struggle to justify or ennoble this 'choice.'"

"It doesn't matter, does it?" said Vance. "Something vital always evades us, and the mind can never answer the questions it propounds. Saying a thing, or not saying it and thinking it, is no different."

"Exactly." The man gave Vance a glance of interrogation. "What thought have you?"

"I was wondering why you were in New York. I saw you at the *Domdaniel* Saturday." Vance's tone had changed.

"I saw you too, though I was not certain. I thought then you might get in touch with me. Your presence that night was not a coincidence. There are no coincidences. A babu word to cloak our reeking ignorance. There is only one pattern in the entire universe of time."

"But your visit to the city. Do I intrude on a secret?"

Owen snarled, and I could feel a chill go down my spine. Then his expression changed to one of sadness.

"I came to see a specialist—Enrick Hofmann."

"Yes. One of the world's greatest cardiologists. You saw him?"

"Two days ago." Owen laughed bitterly. "Doomed! *Mene, mene, tekel, upharsin.*"

Vance merely raised his eyebrows slightly, and drew deeply on his cigarette.

"Thank you," said Owen, "for sparing me the meaningless platitudes." Then he asked suddenly: "Are you a Daniel?"

"Does Belshazzar need an augur?" Vance looked straight at the man... "No, alas! I am no Daniel. Nor am I a Dominic."

Owen chuckled diabolically.

"I was sure you knew!" He wagged his head in satisfaction. "Mirche will die without the faintest suspicion of the jest. He's as ignorant of the *Thousand and One Nights* as he is of Southey and Carlyle.* An illiterate swine!"

"It was a clever idea," said Vance.

"Oh, no; not clever. Merely a bit of humor." Lethargy again seemed to pervade him; his expression became a mask; his hands lay limp on the arms of the chair. He might have been a corpse. There was a long silence; then Vance spoke.

"The handwriting on the wall. Would it comfort you to have me suggest that perhaps all the years throughout infinity are counted and divided?"

"No," Owen snapped. " 'Comfort'—another babu word." Then he went on wistfully: "Eternal recurrence—*resurgam.* The perfect torture." He began to mutter. " 'The sea will begin to wither...an extinct planet...absorbed in the sun... greater suns...the ultimate moment...eternal dispersal of things...billions of years hence...*this same room...*' " He shook himself weakly, and stared at Vance. "Moore was right: it is like madness."

Vance nodded sympathetically.

---

*   Southey used the Domdaniel as the subject of his "Thalaba"; and it
     was Carlyle who made the Domdaniel of the Arabian Nights
     synonymous with a "den of iniquity."

"Yes. Madness. Quite. The moment'ry finite is all we dare face. But there is no finite."

"No, no finite, of course." Owen spoke sepulchrally. "But those billions of years beyond, when the mind returns to infinity...like the endless ripples made by a stone cast in the water. Then we must have cleanliness of spirit. Not now. But then. We must cause no endless ripples... Thank God, I can talk to you."

Again Vance nodded.

"Yes, I quite understand. 'Cleanliness'—I know what you mean. The finite balances itself—that is, we can balance it, even at the last. We can go back clean to endless time. Yes. 'Cleanliness of spirit'—an apposite phrase. No ripples. I wholly agree."

"But not through restitution," Owen said quickly. "No preposterous confessionals."

Vance waved his hand in negation.

"I didn't mean that. Merely a *néant*—a nothingness—after the finite, when there will be no further struggle, no more trying to eliminate the impulses placed in us by the same agency that puts a taboo on our indulging them..."

"That's it!" There was a flicker of animation in Owen's voice; then he lapsed again into languor. The slight gesture of his hand was as graceful as a woman's. But the steely hardness in his gaze remained. "You will see that I cause no ripples, in case...?"

"Yes," returned Vance simply. "If the occasion should ever arise, and I am able to help, you may count on me."

"I trust you... And now, may I speak a moment? I have long wanted to say these things to someone who would understand..."

Vance merely waited, and Owen went on.

"Nothing has the slightest importance—not even life itself. We ourselves can create or smear out human beings—it is all one, whichever we do." He grinned hopelessly. "The rotten futility of all things—the futility of doing anything, even of thinking. Damn the agonizing succession of days we call Life! My temperament has ever drawn me in many directions at once—always the thumbscrew and the rack. Perhaps, after all, to smear souls out is better."

He seemed to shrink as from a ghost; and Vance put in:

"I know the unrest that comes from too much needless activity, with all its multiplying desires."

"The aimless struggle! Yes, yes. The struggle to fit oneself into a mold that differs from one's ancient mold. That is the ultimate curse. The instinct to achieve—faugh! We learn its worthlessness only when it has devoured us. I have been fired by different instincts at different times. They are all lies—cunning, corroding lies. And we think we can subject our instincts to the mind. The mind!" He laughed softly. "The mind's only value is attained when it teaches us that it is useless."

He moved a little, as if a slight involuntary spasm had shaken him.

"Nor can we attribute our distorted instincts to racial memory. There are no races—only one great filthy stream of life flowing out of the primeval slime. The abortive sensualism of primordial animal life lies dormant within all of us. If we suppress it, it manifests itself in cruelty and sadism; if we unleash it, it produces perversions and insanity. There is no answer."

"Man sometimes strives to counteract these horrors by releasing an inner ideal from its abstract conception through visual symbols."

"Symbols themselves are abstractions," came Owen's mordant monotone. "Nor can logic help. Logic leads no man to the truth: logic leads only to insane delusions. The apotheosis of logic:—angels dancing on the point of a needle... But why do I even bother, in this shadow between two infinities? I can give only one answer: the obscene urge to eat well and live well—which, in turn, is an instinct and, therefore, a lie."

"It may go farther back than that instinct," Vance suggested. "It may be an urge brought here when the shadow of life first fell across the path of infinity—the cosmic urge to play a game with life, in order to escape from the stresses and pressures of the finite."

(I now knew that Vance had some very definite—but, to me, obscure—purpose in mind as he talked with this strange, unnatural man before him.)

"Here in this dreamed-out world," said Owen hazily, "one course is no better than another; one person or thing is no more important than any other person or thing. All opposites are interchangeable—creation or slaughter, serenity or torture. Yet vanity seeps through the scabby crust of my congealed metaphysics. Bah!" He hunched himself over and stared at Vance. "There is neither time nor existence here."

"As you say. Infinity is not relatively divisible."

"But there is the terrifying possibility that we can add some factor to the time before us. And if we do, that factor will continue eternally... There must be no pebble thrown. We must cut through this shadow clean."

Owen had closed his eyes, and Vance scrutinized him without expression. Then he said in an almost consoling tone:

"That is wisdom... Yes. Cleanliness of spirit."

Owen nodded with great languor.

"Tomorrow night I sail for South America. Warmth—the ocean...nepenthe, perhaps. I'll be engaged all tomorrow. Things to be done—accounts, a house-cleaning, temporal orderliness. No ripples to follow me for all time. Cleanliness—beyond... You understand?"

"Yes." Vance did not lower his gaze. "I understand. Cessation here, lest there be a 'hound of Heaven'..."

The man's slow eyes opened. He straightened and lighted another cigarette. His strange mood was dissipated, and another look came into his eyes. Throughout this discussion he had not once raised his voice; nor had there been more than the mildest inflection in his words. Yet I felt as if I had been listening to a bitter and passionate tirade.

Owen began speaking now of old books, of his days at Cambridge, of his cultural ambitions as a youth, of his early

study of music. He was steeped in the lore of ancient civiliza-
tions and, to my astonishment, he dwelt with fanatical passion
on the Tibetan *Book of the Dead*. But, strangely enough, he
spoke of himself always with a sense of dualism, as if telling of
someone else. There was a sensitive courtesy in the man, but
somehow he instilled in me a repugnance akin to fear. There
was always an invisible aura about him, like that of a primitive, smouldering beast. I was unwholesomely fascinated by
the man; and I experienced an unmistakable sensation of relief
when Vance stood up to go.

As we parted from him at the door, he said to Vance with
seeming irrelevancy:

"Counted, weighed, divided... You have promised me."

Vance met his gaze directly for a brief moment.

"Thank you," breathed Owen, with a deep bow.

CHAPTER FIFTEEN

An Appalling Accusation
(Tuesday, May 21; 9:30 a.m.)

"YES, MARKHAM, QUITE mad," Vance summa-
rized, as we were finishing breakfast in his apartment the next
morning. "Quite. A poisonous madman, like some foul, crawling
creature. His end is rapidly approaching, and a hideous fear
has wrecked his brain. The sudden anticipation of death has
severed his cord of sanity. He's seeking a hole in which to hide
from the unescapable. But he has nowhere to take cover—only
the mephitic charnel house which his warped brain has erected.
That is his one remaining reality... A vile creature that should
be stamped out as one would destroy a deadly germ. A mental,
moral and spiritual leper. Unclean. Polluted. And I—I—am to
save him from the horrors infinity holds for him!"

"You must have had a pleasant evening with him,"
commented Markham with distaste.

Sergeant Heath, having arrived in answer to an earlier telephone summons from Vance, had listened attentively to the conversation. But he seemed to withdraw into himself when, a few moments later, Gracie Allen came tripping gayly into the library.

She carried a small wooden box, held tightly to her. Behind her was George Burns, diffident and hesitant. Miss Allen explained things buoyantly.

"I just *had* to come, Mr. Vance, to show you my clues. And George had just come to see me; so I brought him along, too. I think he should know how we're getting along. Don't you, Mr. Vance? And mother, *she's* coming over too in a little while. She said she wants to see you, though I can't even *imagine* why."

The girl paused long enough for Vance to present Markham. She accepted him without the suspicion she had previously accorded Heath; and Markham was both fascinated and amused by her lively and irrelevant chatter.

"And now, Mr. Vance," the girl continued, going to the desk and taking the tight cover from the little box she had brought, "I've simply *got* to show you my clues. But I really don't think they're any good, because I didn't know exactly where to look for them. Anyhow..."

She began to display her treasures. Vance humored her and pretended to be greatly interested. Markham, puzzled but smiling, came forward a few steps; and Burns stood, ill at ease, at the other side of the desk. Heath, annoyed by the frivolous interruption, disgustedly lighted a cigar and walked to the window.

"Now here, Mr. Vance, is the exact size of a footprint." Gracie Allen took out a slip of paper with some figures written on it. "It measures just eleven inches long, and the man at the shoe store said that was the length of a number nine-and-a-half shoe—unless it was an English shoe, and then it might be only a number nine. But I don't think he was English—I mean the man with the foot. I think he was a Greek, because he was one of the waiters up at the *Domdaniel.* You see, I went up there because that's where you said the dead man was found. And I waited a long time for someone to come out of the kitchen to make a footprint; and then, when no one was looking, I measured it..."

She put the paper to one side.

"And now, here's a piece of blotter that I took from the desk in Mr. Puttle's office at lunch-time yesterday, when he wasn't there. And I held it to a mirror, but all it says is '4 dz Sw So,' just like I wrote it out again here. All that means is, 'four dozen boxes of sandalwood soap.'..."

She brought out two or three other useless odds and ends which she explained in amusing detail, as she placed them beside the others.

Vance did not interrupt her during this diverting, but pathetic, display. But Burns, who was growing nervous and exasperated at the girl's unnecessary wasting of time, finally seemed to lose his patience and burst out:

"Why don't you show the gentlemen the almonds you have there, and get this silly business over with?"

"I haven't any almonds, George. There's only one thing left in the box, and that hasn't *anything* to do with it. I was just sort of practicing when I got that clue——"

"But something smells like bitter almond to *me*."

Vance suddenly became seriously interested.

"What else have you in the box, Miss Allen?" he asked.

She giggled as she took out the last item—a slightly bulging and neatly sealed envelope.

"It's only an old cigarette," she said. "And that's a good joke on George. He's always smelling the funniest odors. I guess he can't help it."

She tore away the corner of the envelope and let a flattened and partly broken cigarette slip into her hand. At first glimpse, I would have said that it had not been lighted, but then I noticed its charred end, as if a few inhalations had been taken on it. Vance took the cigarette and held it gingerly near his nose.

tie together the annoyin' factors that have robbed me of sweet sleep—Mirche's ready admission concerning his secret door; the hatred I glimpsed in the eyes of the Lorelei; the mystic lore of the Tofanas; and the presence of the 'Owl' at the *Domdaniel* Saturday night. It might explain the subtle implications in the name of the café. It might even justify the Sergeant's haunting hypothesis of a criminal ring. It might, conceivably, elucidate Mr. Burns' migrat'ry cigarette case with its scent of jonquille. And there are other things now baffling me that might be assembled into a consistent whole... My word, Markham! it has the most amazin' possibilities. Let me have my hasheesh dream. A pattern is forming at last in my whirling brain; and it is the first coherent design that has invaded my enfevered imagination since Sabbath eve. With the droll premise that the cigarette was adequately poisoned, I can force a score of hitherto recalcitrant elements into line—or, rather, they tumble into line themselves, like the tiny colored particles in a kaleidoscope."

"Vance, for the love of Heaven! You're simply creating a new and more preposterous fantasy to explain away your first fantasy." Markham's severe tone quickly sobered Vance.

"Yes, you're quite right," he said. "I shall, of course, send the cigarette at once to Doremus for analysis. And it will probably reveal nothing. As you say. Frankly, I don't understand how the odor could have remained on the cigarette so long, unless one of the combining poisons acted as a fixator and retarded volatilization... But, Markham, I do want—I *need*—a dead man who was killed in Riverdale last Saturday."

Gracie Allen had been looking from one to the other in a bewildered daze.

"Oh, *now* I bet I understand!" she exclaimed exultantly. "You *really* think the cigarette could have *killed* somebody... But I never *heard* of anyone dying from smoking just *one* cigarette."

"Not an ordin'ry cigarette, my dear," Vance explained patiently. "It is only possible if the cigarette has been dipped in some terrible poison."

"Why, that's awful, if it's really true," she mused. "And up in Riverdale, of all places! It's so pretty and quiet up there…"

Her eyes began to grow wide, and finally she exclaimed: "But I bet I know who the dead man was! *I bet I know!*"

"What in the world are you talking about?" Vance laughed and looked at her with puzzled eyes. "Who do you think it was?"

She looked back at him searchingly for a few moments, and then said:

"Why, it was Benny the Buzzard!"

Sergeant Heath stiffened suddenly, his mouth agape. "Where did *you* ever hear that name, Miss?" he almost shouted.

"Why—why—" She stammered, taken aback by his vehemence. "Mr. Vance told me all about him."

"Mr. Vance told you—?"

"Of course he did!" the girl said defiantly. "*That's* how I know that Benny the Buzzard was killed in Riverdale."

"Killed in Riverdale?" The Sergeant looked dazed. "And maybe you know who killed him, too?"

"I should say I do know… It was *Mr. Vance himself!*"

CHAPTER SIXTEEN

Another Shock
(Tuesday, May 21; 10:30 a.m.)

THE APPALLING ACCUSATION came like a paralyzing shock. It was several moments before I could collect myself sufficiently to see the logic behind it. It was the natural outcome of the story which Vance had built up for the girl the afternoon he had first met her.

Markham, with only meager details of that rustic encounter and knowing nothing of the tall tale spun by Vance, must have recalled immediately the conversation at the Bellwood Country Club, in which Vance had expressed his extravagant ideas as to how Pellinzi should be disposed of.

Heath, too, flabbergasted by the girl's announcement, must have remembered that Friday-night dinner; and it was not beyond reason to assume that he now held some hazy suspicion of Vance's guilt.

Vance himself was temporarily astounded. Weightier matters had undoubtedly crowded the entire Riverdale episode from his mind for the moment; but now he suddenly realized how Gracie Allen's accusation took on the color of plausibility.

Markham approached the girl with an austere frown.

"That is a grave charge you have just made, Miss Allen," he said. His gruff tone indicated the intangible doubts in the recesses of his mind.

"My word, Markham!" Vance put in, not without annoyance. "Please glance about you. This is not a courtroom."

"I know exactly where I am," retorted Markham testily. "Let me handle this matter—it's full of dynamite." He turned back to the girl. "Tell me just why you say Mr. Vance killed Benny the Buzzard."

"Why, *I* didn't say it—that is, I didn't make it up out of my own head. I just sort of repeated it."

Although she obviously did not regard the situation as serious, it was evident that Markham's sternness had disturbed her.

"It was *Mr. Vance* who said it. He said it when I first met him in Riverdale beside the road that runs along a big white wall—last Saturday afternoon, when I was with—that is, I went there with—"

Markham, aware of the girl's nervousness, smiled reassuringly and spoke in an altered manner.

"There's nothing for you to worry about, Miss Allen," he said. "Just tell me the whole story, exactly as it happened."

"Oh!" she exclaimed, a brighter note returning to her voice. "Why didn't you tell me *that's* what you wanted?... All right, I *will* tell you. Well, I went up to Riverdale last Saturday afternoon—we don't have to work at the factory on Saturday afternoons, ever; Mr. Doolson is very nice about that. I went up with Mr. Puttle—he's one of our salesmen, you know; but I *really* don't think he's as good as some of the other In-O-Scent salesmen. Do you, George?"

She turned momentarily to Burns, but did not wait for a reply.

"Well, anyhow, George wanted me to go somewhere else with him; but I thought maybe it *might* be best if I went to Riverdale with Mr. Puttle, especially as he was taking me to dinner that night. And I thought maybe he might get angry if I didn't go to Riverdale with him, and then he wouldn't take me to dinner; so I didn't go with George, but I went to Riverdale with Mr. Puttle. Don't you think maybe I was right? Anyhow, that's how I happened to be at Riverdale... Well, we got to Riverdale—I often go there—I think it's just *lovely* up there. But it's an *awful* long walk from Broadway—and then Mr. Puttle went to look for a nunnery—"

"Please, Miss Allen," interrupted Markham, with admirable composure; "tell me how you happened to meet Mr. Vance, and what he said to you."

"Oh, I was coming to that... Mr. Vance came falling over the wall. And I asked him what he'd been doing. And he said he'd been killing a man. And I said what was the man's name. And he said Benny the Buzzard."

Markham sighed with impatience.

"Can you tell me a few other things, Miss Allen, about the—incident?"

"All right. As I already told you, Mr. Vance came falling over the wall, just behind where I was sitting—no, excuse me, I wasn't sitting, because somebody had just thrown a cigarette at me—that cigarette up there on the mantelpiece—only it was burning—and I was standing up, shaking it off my dress, when I heard Mr. Vance fall. He seemed in an *awful* hurry, too. I told him about the cigarette, and he said maybe he had thrown it himself; although *I* thought someone had thrown it out of a big automobile that had just whizzed by. Anyhow, Mr. Vance told me to get a new dress and it wouldn't cost me anything because he was sorry. And then he sat down and smoked some more cigarettes."

She took a deep breath and hurried on.

"And then was when I asked him what he was doing on the other side of the wall, and he said that he had just killed a very bad man named Benny the Buzzard. He said he did it because this Mr. Buzzard had broken out of jail and was going to murder a friend of his—that is, I mean a friend of Mr. Vance's. Mr. Vance was all mussed up, and he certainly *looked* like he might have just killed somebody. I was even scared of him myself for a while. But I got all over that…"

She took a moment to survey Vance up and down, as if making a sartorial comparison.

"Well now, let's see, where was I? Oh, yes… He was running away in a *terrible* hurry, because he said he didn't want *anybody* to know about his killing the man. But he told *me*. I guess he saw right away he could trust me. But I don't know why he was worried about it, because he said he thought he had done right to save his friend from danger. Anyhow, he asked me not to tell *anybody*; and I promised. But he just now asked me to tell what I meant about the dead man in Riverdale, so I guess he meant I didn't have to keep my promise any more. So that's why I'm telling you."

Markham's astonishment rose as the girl rambled on. When she completed her recital and looked round for approval, the District Attorney turned to Vance.

"Good Heavens, Vance! Is this story actually true?"

"I fear so," Vance admitted, shrugging.

"But why—how did you come to tell her such a story?"

"The balmy weather, perhaps. In the spring, y' know…"

"But," demanded the girl, "aren't you going to *arrest* him?"

"No—I—" Markham was left floundering.

"Why not?" the girl insisted. "I'll bet I know why! I'll bet you think that you can't arrest a detective. I thought so, too—once. But Sunday I asked a policeman; and he said *of course* you can arrest a detective."

"Yes; you can arrest a detective," smiled Markham, "if you know that he has broken a law. But I have very grave doubts that Mr. Vance has actually killed a man."

"But he said so *himself.* And how else could you know? I *really* didn't think he was guilty either—at first. I thought he was just telling me a romantic story because I *love* romantic stories! But then, Mr. Vance *himself* just said—right here in this very room—you heard him—he said that there was a dead man killed with the cigarette in Riverdale last Saturday. And he was *very serious* about it—I could tell by the way he acted and talked. It wasn't *at all* like he was making up a romantic story again..."

She stopped abruptly and looked at the befuddled Mr. Burns. Judging from her expression, another idea had come into her head. She turned back to Markham with renewed seriousness.

"But you *really* ought to arrest Mr. Vance," she said with definiteness. "Even if he *isn't* guilty. I guess I don't really think he *is* guilty myself. He's been so *awfully* nice to me. But still I think you ought to arrest him just the same. You see, what I mean is that you can pretend that you believe he killed this man in Riverdale. And *then* everything would be all right for George. And Mr. Vance wouldn't care a bit—I *know he wouldn't.* Would you, Mr. Vance?"

"What in Heaven's name are you driving at now?" asked Markham.

Vance smiled.

"I know exactly what she means, Markham." He turned to Miss Allen. "But really, y' know, my arrest wouldn't help Mr. Burns."

"Oh, *yes it would,*" she insisted. "I *know* it would. Because there's somebody following him wherever he goes. And George says he bets it's a detective of some kind. And all the policemen around George's hotel look at him in the *strangest* way. There's just *lots* of people, I bet, who think George is guilty—like after they came to the house and took him away in a wagon to jail, and everything. George told me *all* about it, and it worries him *terribly.* He isn't at all like he used to be. He can't sleep very well; and he doesn't smell so good. So how can he work?... You don't know how *awful* it is, Mr. Vance. But if *you* got arrested, then everybody would think that *you* were guilty and they wouldn't bother George any more; and he could go back to work and be just like he used to be. And then, after a while, they'd find the *real* person, and everything would be all right for everybody."

She stopped to catch her breath; then quickly ran on with almost fiery determination.

"And *that's* why I think you ought to arrest Mr. Vance. *And if you don't*, I'm going to call up the newspapers and tell them *everything* he said and all about Benny the Buzzard, and how he wasn't killed at the *Domdaniel* at all, but somewheres else. I'll bet they'll print it, too. Especially as Mr. Puttle was standing just behind the tree when Mr. Vance was talking to me, and he heard *everything.* And if they don't believe *me*, they'll believe Mr. Puttle. And if they don't believe *him*, they'll have to believe the two of us together. And then I'm *sure* they'll print it. And everybody'll be so interested in a famous man like Mr. Vance being guilty, that they won't bother about George any more. Don't you see what I mean?"

There was the zealous resolution of the crusader in her eyes; and her disorganized phrases pulsated with an unreasoning passion to help the man she loved.

"Good God, Chief!" blurted Heath. "There sure *is* dynamite there. *You said it!*"

Vance moved lethargically in his chair and looked at Heath with a satirical smile.

"You see what you and your shadowing Mr. Tracy have got me in for, Sergeant?"

"Sure I do!" Heath took a step toward Miss Allen. His perturbation was almost comical. "See here, Miss," he blustered. "Listen to me a minute. You're all wrong. You got everything mixed up. We don't know there was a murder in Riverdale. We don't know nothing about that, see? We only know about the dead guy in the café. And he wasn't the Buzzard; he was your brother—"

He stopped short with a jerk, and his face went red.

"*Holy Mackerel!* I'm sorry as hell, Mr. Vance."

Vance rose quickly and went to the girl's side. She had her hands to her face in a spasm of uncontrollable laughter.

"My brother? My *brother?*" Then as quickly as she had burst into mirth, she sobered. "You can't fool me that way, Mr. Officer."

Vance stepped back.

"Tell me,"—a sudden new note came into his voice—"what do you mean by that, Miss Allen?"

"*My brother's in jail!*"

CHAPTER SEVENTEEN

Fingerprints
(Tuesday, May 21; 11:30 a.m.)

IT WAS AT this moment that Mrs. Allen, serene and self-effacing, was guided into the room by Currie.

Vance turned quickly and welcomed her with but the briefest of greetings.

"Is it true, Mrs. Allen," he asked, "that your son is not dead?"

"Yes, it is true, Mr. Vance. That's why I came over here."

Vance nodded with an understanding smile and, leading the woman to a chair, asked her to explain more fully.

"You see, sir," she began in a colorless voice, "Philip was arrested over near Hackensack that awful night, after he had given up his job at the café. He was with another boy in an automobile, and a policeman got in and told this other boy—it's Stanley Smith I mean, a friend of Philip's—to drive to the police station. He accused them of stealing the car; and then, when they were on the way to the jail, the policeman said that it was the same car that had just killed an old man and run off—you know, what you call a hit-and-run murder. And this frightened Philip terribly, because he didn't know what Stanley might have done before they met. And then, when the car stopped for a light, Philip jumped out and ran away. The policeman shot at him, but he wasn't caught."

Vance nodded sympathetically.

"Then Philip telephoned to me—I could tell how frightened he was—and said that the police were after him and that he was going somewhere to hide... Oh, I was so terribly worried, Mr. Vance, with the poor miserable boy so scared, and hiding—you know, a fugitive from justice. And then when you came that night I thought you were looking for him; but when you told me my boy was dead, you can imagine—"

Heath leaped forward.

"But you said that was your son down at the morgue!" He flung the words at her.

"No, I didn't, Mr. Officer," the woman said simply.

"The hell you didn't!" bellowed Heath.

"Sergeant!" Vance held up his hand. "Mrs. Allen is quite correct... If you think back, you will remember she did not once say it was her son. I'm afraid we said it for her, because we thought it was true." He smiled wistfully.

"But she fainted, didn't she?" pursued Heath.

"I fainted from joy, Mr. Officer," explained the woman, "when I saw it wasn't really Philip."

Heath was by no means satisfied.

"But—but you—didn't say it *wasn't* your son. And you let us think—"

Again Vance checked him.

"I believe I understand exactly why Mrs. Allen let us think it was her son. She knew we represented the police, and she also knew her son was hiding from them. And when she saw that we believed her son was dead, she was very glad to let us think so, imagining that would end the hunt for Philip... Isn't that true, Mrs. Allen?"

"Yes, Mr. Vance." The woman nodded calmly. "And I naturally didn't want you to tell Gracie that Philip was dead, because then I would have to tell her that he was hiding from the police; and that would have made her very unhappy. But I thought that maybe in a few days everything would come out all right; and then I would tell you. Anyhow, I thought you would find out before long that it really wasn't Philip."

She looked up with a faint, sad smile.

"And everything *did* come out all right, just as I hoped and prayed—and *knew*—it would."

"We're all very happy that it did," said Vance. "But tell us just how everything has come out all right."

"Why, this morning," resumed Mrs. Allen, "Stanley Smith came to the house to ask for Philip. And when I told him that Philip was still hiding, he said that everything had been a mistake; and how his uncle came to the jail and proved to the police that the car was not stolen, and how it was a different car that had run over the old man... So I told Gracie all about it right away, and went to take the wonderful news to my son and bring him back home..."

"How come then,"—the Sergeant's continued exasperation was evident in his manner—"if you told your daughter all about it, that she said just now her brother was in jail?"

Mrs. Allen smiled timidly.

"Oh, he is. You see, Saturday was such a warm night that Philip had his coat off in the car; and he left it there. That's how the police knew who he was, because he had his work-check in the pocket. So he went to the jail in Hackensack this morning to get his coat. And he's coming home for lunch."

Vance laughed in spite of himself, and gave Gracie Allen a mischievous look.

"And I'll warrant it was a *black* coat."

"Oh, Mr. Vance!" the girl exclaimed ecstatically. "What a *wonderful* detective you are! How could you *possibly tell* what color Philip's coat was 'way over there across the river?"

Vance chuckled and then became suddenly serious. "And now I must ask you all to go," he said, "and prepare for Philip's homecoming."

At this point Markham intervened.

"But what about that story you were threatening to tell to the newspapers, Miss Allen? I couldn't permit anything like that."

George Burns, with a broad grin on his face, answered the District Attorney.

"Gracie won't do that, Mr. Markham. You see, I'm perfectly happy now, and I'm going back to work tomorrow morning. I really wasn't worrying about being guilty or about having anybody following me around. But I had to tell that to Gracie—and Mr. Doolson—because you made me promise that I wouldn't say a word about Philip. And it was Philip being dead and Gracie not knowing, and everything, that made me feel so terribly bad that I just couldn't get any sleep or do any work."

"Isn't that *wonderful!*" Miss Allen clapped her hands, and then glanced slyly at Vance. "I didn't *really* want you to go to jail, Mr. Vance—except to help George. So I give you my promise I won't say *one word* to anybody about your confession. And you know I *always* keep a promise."

As Mrs. Allen was departing with her daughter and Burns, she gave Vance a look of shy apology.

"I do hope, sir," she said, "that you don't think I did wrong in deceiving you about that poor boy—downtown."

Vance took her hand in his.

"I certainly think nothing of the kind. You acted as any mother would have acted, had she been as clever and as quick-witted as you."

He raised her hand to his lips, and then closed the door after the trio.

"And now, Sergeant,"—his whole manner changed—"get busy! Call Tracy up here, and then try to have that dead fellow identified by his fingerprints."

"You don't have to tell me to get busy, sir," returned Heath, hurrying to the window. He beckoned frantically to the man across the street. Then he turned back into the room, and on his way to the telephone, he halted abruptly, as if a sudden thought had left him motionless.

"Say, Mr. Vance," he asked, "what makes you think his fingerprints'll be on file?"

Vance gave him a searching, significant look.

"You may be greatly surprised, Sergeant."

"Mother o' God!" breathed Heath in an awed tone, as he dashed to the instrument in the hall.

While the Sergeant was talking with almost incoherent agitation to the Bureau, Tracy came in. Vance sent him at once to Doremus' laboratory with the sealed envelope on the mantel.

In a few minutes Heath returned to the library.

"Are those babies on the job!" He rubbed his hands together energetically. "They'll sure burn up shoe-leather getting those fingerprints and checking up in the file. And if they don't call me back in an hour, I'll go down there and wring their thick necks!" He collapsed in a chair as if exhausted by the mere thought of the speed and activity he had demanded.

Vance himself now telephoned Doremus, explaining that an immediate report on the cigarette was essential.

It was nearly noon, and we chatted aimlessly for another hour. There was a tension in the atmosphere, and the conversation was like a cloak deliberately thrown over the inner thoughts of these three diverse men.

As the clock over the mantel pointed to one, the telephone rang, and Vance answered it.

"There was no difficulty with that analysis," he informed us, as he hung up the receiver. "The efficient Doremus found in the cigarette the same elusive combination of poisons that bothered him so frightfully Sunday evening... My jumbled story, Markham, is at last beginning to take form."

He had barely finished speaking when the telephone rang again, and it was Heath who now dashed into the hall. As he came back into the library after a few moments, he stumbled against a small Renaissance stand near the door and sent it sprawling.

"All right, I'm excited. So what?" The Sergeant's eyes were staring. "Who do you think the guy was? But hell! You knew it already, Mr. Vance. It's our old chum, Benny the Buzzard!... And maybe those boys down in Pittsburgh wasn't nuts! And maybe the Buzzard didn't hop straight from Nomenica to New York, just like I said he would!... Laugh that one off, Mr. Markham."

Heath's excitement was such that it temporarily over-weighed even his respectful manner toward the District Attorney.

"What'll we do next, Mr. Vance?"

"I should say, Sergeant, that the first thing is for you to sit down. Calm. A most necess'ry virtue."

Heath readily complied, and Vance turned to Markham.

"I believe this is still my case, so to speak. You most magnanimously presented it to me, to rid yourself of my chatter last Saturday night. I must, therefore, now ask a further indulgence."

Markham waited in silence.

"The time has come when I must act with dispatch," Vance continued. "The whole case, Markham, has become quite clear; the various fragments have fitted themselves together into a rather amazing mosaic. But there are still one or two blank spaces. And I believe that Mirche, if properly approached, can supply the missin' pieces..."

Heath broke in.

"I'm beginning to get you, sir. You think that Mirche's identification of the Buzzard was deliberately phony?"

"No—oh, no, Sergeant. Mirche was quite sincere—and with very good reason. He was genuinely stunned by the appearance of the dead body in his office that night."

"Then I *don't* get you, sir," said Heath, disgruntled.

"What's the indulgence you're after, Vance?" Markham asked impatiently.

"I merely wish to make an arrest."

"But I certainly do not propose to let you get the District. Attorney's office into hot water. We must wait until the case is solved."

"Ah! but it *is* solved," Vance returned blandly. "And you may toddle along with me, to protect the sanctity of your office. In fact, I'd be charmed with your company."

"Come to the point." Markham spoke irritably. "Just what is it you want to do?"

Vance leaned forward and spoke with precision.

"I desire most fervently to go to the *Domdaniel* as soon as possible this afternoon. I desire to have two men—let us say Hennessey and Burke—standing guard in the passageway outside the secret door. I then desire to proceed with you and the Sergeant to the front door on the balcony, and demand entry. Then I will take action—under your vigilant and restraining eye, of course."

"But, good Heavens, Vance! Mirche may not be waiting in his office for your visit. He may have other plans for his afternoon's diversion."

"That," remarked Vance, "is a chance we must take. But I have sufficient reason to believe that Mirche's office is a beehive of secret activity today. And I would be rather astonished if the Lorelei—and Owen, too—were not there. Tonight, y' know, Owen is sailin' for the southern hemisphere, and this is his day for closin' up his mundane affairs here. You and the Sergeant have long suspected that the *Domdaniel* is the headquarters for all sorts of naughty goings on. You need doubt no more, my Markham."

The District Attorney pondered a moment.

"It sounds preposterous and futile," he asserted. "Unless you have some cryptic grounds for such an absurd course... However, as you say, I'll be there myself to guard against any imbecile indiscretion on your part... Very well." He capitulated.

Vance nodded with satisfaction and looked at the bewildered Heath.

"And by the by, Sergeant, we may possibly hear rumors of your friends Rosa and Tony."

"The Tofanas!" Heath sat up alertly. "I knew it. That cigarette job is right up Tony's alley..."

Vance outlined his plan to the Sergeant. Heath was to arrange with Joe Hanley, the doorman, to give a signal if Mirche should quit the dining room by the rear exit. Hennessey and Burke were to be instructed regarding their post and duties. And Markham and Vance and Heath were to wait in the rooming-house opposite, whence they could see either Hanley's signal or Mirche himself entering his office by way of the balcony.

However, many of the elaborate and intricate preparations proved unnecessary; for Vance's theory and prognostications with reference to the situation that afternoon were entirely correct.

CHAPTER EIGHTEEN

Jonquille and Rose
(Tuesday. May 21; 3 p.m.)

AT THREE O'CLOCK that afternoon Joe Hanley, who had been watching for us, came to the corner of Seventh Avenue and informed us that Mirche had entered his office shortly after noon, and that neither he nor Miss Del Marr had been seen in the café since then.

We found the shades at the narrow windows drawn; the door to the office was locked; nor was there any response to our insistent knocking.

"Open up, you!" Heath bawled ferociously. "Or have I gotta bust in the door?" Then he remarked to us: "I guess that'll scare 'em, if anybody's there."

Soon we could hear the sound of scuffling and angry voices inside; and a few moments later the door was unlocked for us by Hennessey.

"It's okay now, sir," he said to Markham. "They tried to sneak out the wall door, but Burke and I forced 'em back."

As we stepped across the threshold, a strange sight met our eyes. Burke stood with his back against the little secret door, his gun pointed significantly at the startled Mirche who was but a few steps away. Dixie Del Marr, also in line with Burke's gun, was leaning against the desk, looking at us with an expression of cold resignation. In one of the leather chairs sat Owen, smiling faintly with calm cynicism. He seemed entirely dissociated from the general tableau, like a spectator viewing a theatrical scene which offended his intellect by its absurdity. He looked neither to right nor left; and it was not until we were well within range of his somnolent gaze, that he made the slightest movement.

When he caught sight of Vance, however, he rose wearily and bowed in formal greeting.

"What futile effort," he complained. Then he sat down again with a mild sigh, like one who feels he must remain to the end of a distasteful drama.

Hennessey closed the door and stood alertly watching the occupants of the room. Burke, at a sign from Heath, let his hand fall to his side, but maintained a stolid vigilance.

"Sit down, Mr. Mirche," said Vance. "Merely a little discussion."

As the white and frightened man dropped into a chair at the desk, Vance bowed politely to Miss Del Marr.

"It isn't necess'ry for you to stand."

"I prefer it," the woman said in a hard tone. "I've been sitting and waiting, as it were, for three years now."

Vance accepted her cryptic remark without comment, and turned his attention back to Mirche.

"We have discussed preferences in foods and wines at some length," he said casually; "and I was wondering what private brand of cigarettes you favor."

The man seemed paralyzed with fear. But quickly he recovered himself; a semblance of his former suavity returned. He made a croaking noise intended for a laugh.

"I have no private brand," he declared. "I always smoke—"

"No, no," Vance interrupted. "I mean your *very* private brand—reserved for the elect."

Mirche laughed again, and gestured broadly with upturned palms to indicate the question conveyed no meaning to him.

"By the by," Vance went on, "in medieval times—when Madam Tofana and other famous poisoners flourished—there were many flowers which, romantic legend tells us, would bring death with a single whiff... Strange how these legends persist and how examples of their apparent authenticity crop up in modern times. One wonders, don't y' know, whether the old secrets of alchemy have indeed been preserved to the present day. Of course, such speculations are absurd in the light of modern science."

"I don't see your point." Mirche spoke with an attempt at injured dignity. "Nor do I understand this outrageous invasion of my privacy."

Vance ignored the man for a moment and addressed Miss Del Marr.

"You have perhaps lost an unusual cigarette case of checkerboard design? When it was found it had the scent of jonquille and rose. A vagrant association—it recalled you, Miss Del Marr."

No change was detectable in the woman's hard expression, although she hesitated perceptibly before answering.

"It isn't mine. I believe, though, I know the case you mean. I saw it in this office last Saturday; and that evening Mr. Mirche showed it to me. He had carried it for hours in his pocket—perhaps that's how it took on the odor. Where did you find it, Mr. Vance? I was told it had been left here by one of the café employees... Maybe Mr. Mirche could—"

"I know nothing of such a cigarette case," Mirche stated bluntly. There was a startled energy in his words. He threw a defiant glance at the woman, but her back was to him.

"It doesn't matter, does it?" said Vance. "Only a passing thought."

His eyes were still on Miss Del Marr; and he spoke to her again.

"You know, of course, that Benny Pellinzi is dead."

"Yes—I know." Her words carried no emotion.

"Strange coincidence about that. Or, mayhap, just a vagary of mine." Vance spoke as if he were merely making some matter-of-fact point. "Pellinzi died last Saturday afternoon, shortly after he would have had time to reach New York. At about that time I happened to be wandering in the woods in Riverdale. And as I started to retrace my steps homeward, a large car drove swiftly by. Later I learned that a lighted cigarette had been thrown from that car, almost at the very spot where I had stood. It was a most peculiar cigarette, Miss Del Marr. Only a few puffs had been taken on it. But that wasn't its only peculiarity. There was a deadly poison in it, too—the modern equivalent of the fabulous poisoned flowers that figured in medieval tragedies. And yet, it had been carelessly tossed away on a public highway..."

"A stupid act," came in soft, caustic tones from Owen.

"Fortuitous, let us say—from the finite point of view. Inevitable, really." Vance also spoke softly. "There is only one pattern in all the universe."

"Yes," said Owen with arctic vagueness. "Stupidity is one of the compositional lines."

Vance did not turn. He was still scrutinizing the woman.

"May I continue, Miss Del Marr?" he asked. "Or does my story bore you?"

She gave no indication that she had heard his query.

"The cigarette case I mentioned," Vance went on, "was found on Pellinzi's body. But there were no cigarettes in it. And it had no pungent aroma of the bitter almond—only the sweet scent of jonquille and rose... But Pellinzi was poisoned as by the smelling of an odor. And again there crops up the deadly agent of ancient romance... Strange—is it not?—how the fancy conjures up such remote associations... Poor Pellinzi must have believed and trusted in his assassin. But all that his faith encountered was treachery and death."

Vance paused. There was a tenseness in the small room. Only Owen seemed unconcerned. He looked straight ahead, with a hopeless detached expression, a sneer distorting his cruel mouth.

When Vance spoke again, his manner had changed: there was brusque severity in his voice.

"But perhaps I am not so fanciful, after all. Whom else but you, Miss Del Marr, would Pellinzi first have told of his safe arrival in New York? And how could he have known, these past few years, that someone else had sought and found a response in a heart which had once belonged to him? You have a large enclosed car, Miss Del Marr—a secret trip to Riverdale would have been an easy matter for you. The cigarette case, with your subtle fragrance, was found on him. Love changes, and is cruel..."

An icy chuckle came from Owen. His eyebrows went up slightly. The sneer on his lips changed to the faint semblance of a smile.

"Very clever, Mr. Vance," he muttered. "Admirable, in fact. Patterns within patterns. How easily man is deceived by fantasms!"

"The deceptive order of chaos," said Vance.

Owen nodded almost imperceptibly. His face again became a satirical mask.

"Yes," he breathed. "You, too, have a sense of esoteric humor."

"I doubt," murmured Vance, "that Miss Del Marr appreciates the humor of death."

A strangled moan burst from the woman's throat. She collapsed into a chair and covered her face with her hands.

"Oh, God!" It was the first break in her metallic composure.

A long silence followed. Mirche looked for a moment at Vance and back again at the woman. His face had regained some of its color, but a haunted fear shone in his eyes—a fear as of a malignant ghost whose shape he could not determine. I knew that questions he dared not utter were crowding to his lips.

Slowly the woman raised her head; her hands dropped to her lap and lay there in an attitude of listless dejection. The venomous hardness of her nature regained control. She was about to speak; but she, too, checked the impulse, as if the gauge of her emotions had not yet reached the point of release.

Vance slowly lighted one of his *Régies.* After one or two puffs, he spoke again to the woman, and his words sounded lackadaisical, as if he were putting a question of no particular moment.

"There is still one thing that puzzles me, Miss Del Marr... Why did you bring the dead Pellinzi back here to this office?"

The woman sat like a marble image, while a disdainful cackle broke from Mirche.

"Are you referring, Mr. Vance," he asked, in his erstwhile pompous manner, "to the man found dead in this office? I'm beginning to understand your interest in the unfortunate episode here Saturday night. But I fear you have permitted your imagination to get the better of you. The body found here was that of one of the café helpers."

"Yes. I know whom you mean, Mr. Mirche. Philip Allen." Vance spoke smoothly. "As you said that night. And I have no doubt that you believed it, and still believe it. But seeming facts act strangely at times. A pattern is prone to change its design in the most incredible manner... Is it not true, Mr. Owen?"

"Always true," replied the quiet spectator in the chair. "Confusion. We are victims..."

"What are you two driving at?" asked Mirche, half rising from his chair, as a dawning fear came into his eyes.

"The truth is, Mr. Mirche," said Vance, "Philip Allen is quite alive. After you had discharged him and he accidentally left a cigarette case here which did not belong to him, Philip Allen did *not* return to this office."

"Ridiculous!" Mirche had lost his suavity. "How else could he—?"

"It was Benny Pellinzi who lay dead here that night!"

At this announcement Mirche dropped suddenly back into his chair, and stared with hopeless defiance at the man before him. But the facts had not yet arranged themselves in his mind; and he began to protest anew.

"That's absurd—utterly absurd! I saw Allen's body myself. And I identified it."

"Oh, I don't question the sincerity of your identification." Vance moved closer to the dazed man. His tone was almost honeyed. "You had every reason to think that it was Philip Allen. He is the same size as Pellinzi. He has the same facial contours and coloring, and that day he was wearing the same kind of unobtrusive black clothes in which Pellinzi was sent to his death. You had just talked with Philip Allen in your office a few hours earlier, and, as you said to me yesterday, you were not surprised that he should have come back here. Moreover, death by poison changes the look in the eyes, the whole general appearance of the face. And, furthermore, wasn't Pellinzi the last person in the world you would have expected to find in your office on that particular night? Yes, the last person in the world..."

"But why—" stammered Mirche, "why should Pellinzi have been the last person I would have expected? I knew by the papers that the man had escaped. And it was wholly possible that he would have been fool enough to come to me for help."

"No—oh, no. I do not mean just that, Mr. Mirche," Vance returned quietly. "I had another and more cogent reason for knowing you would not expect to find Pellinzi here that night... *You knew he was dead in Riverdale.*"

"How could I have known that he was dead?" shouted the frantic man, leaping to his feet. "You yourself said it was Dixie Del Marr to whom he would have appealed first, and—her car—her trip to Riverdale—Bah!... You can't intimidate me!"

"Then take it more calmly, Dan," said Owen petulantly. "There's far too much upheaval in this putrid world. Confusion wearies me."

"Again I fear you have misunderstood me, Mr. Mirche." Vance ignored Owen's complaint to his frightened henchman. "I meant merely that Miss Del Marr must have informed you. I am sure you two have no secrets from each other. Complete mutual trust, even in crime. And, knowing that Pellinzi was dead in Riverdale, and that your—shall we say, partner?—would hardly bring the body here, how could you imagine that the dead man in this office that night was Pellinzi? How natural to make a mistake in identity! Y' see: it *couldn't* be Pellinzi; therefore, it must be someone else. And how readily—and logically—Philip Allen came to your mind... But it *was* Pellinzi."

"How do you know it was Benny—?" Mirche was floundering, dazed by some inner mental vision. "You're trying to trick me." Then he almost shrieked: "I tell you, it couldn't have been the Buzzard!"

"Ah, yes. An error on your part." Vance spoke with quiet authority. "No possible doubt. Fingerprints don't lie. You may ask Sergeant Heath, or the District Attorney. Or you may phone the Police Department and satisfy yourself."

"Fool!" snapped Owen, his drowsy eyes on Mirche with a look of unutterable disgust. He turned to Vance. "After all, how futile it is—this devilish dream—this shadow across..." His voice trailed off.

Mirche was staring at some distant point beyond the confines of the room, alone with his thoughts, striving to assemble a disrupted mass of facts.

"But," he mumbled, as if protesting weakly against some inevitable shapeless nemesis, "Miss Del Marr saw the body here, and..."

He lapsed again into calculating silence; and then a deep flush slowly mounted his features, gradually intensifying in color till it seemed the blood must suffocate him. The muscles of his neck tightened; globules of sweat suddenly appeared on his forehead.

Stiffly, and as if with effort, the man turned toward Miss Del Marr, and in a voice of seething hatred, spat out at her a foul and bestial epithet.

CHAPTER NINETEEN

Through the Shadow
(Tuesday. May 21; 4 p.m.)

AGAIN SOME POWERFUL emotion broke through Dixie Del Marr's stony calm. A violent primitive passion blazed in her. She rose and faced Mirche, and her words came like an ineluctable torrent.

"Of course, you filthy creature, I let them think that the dead man in this office—the man you had killed—was Philip Allen. A few more days of doubt and torture for you—what did it matter? I had already waited years to avenge Benny. Oh, I knew only too well your treachery had sent him to prison for twenty years. And I could say nothing to save him. There was only one way for me to square the injustice. I must wait silently, patiently— I knew the moment would come some day... You liked me—you wanted me. That thought was already in your beastly mind when you let Benny get sent up. So I played up to you—I helped you in your rotten schemes. I flattered you. I did what you told me to. And all the time I loved Benny. But I waited…"

She gave a bitter laugh.

"Three years is a long time. And the moment for which I had waited came too late. But I console myself with the thought that Benny's death was a merciful end. He couldn't hope for anything, even when he had managed to break jail. He'd always have been hounded by the police. But he went mad in his cell, mad enough to think he could find real freedom from the prison where your dirty double-crossing had put him."

Irresistible fury drove her on.

"But Benny never knew of your treachery. He thought you his friend. And he came to you for help. But, thank God, he called me too when he got back last Saturday. He told me he had phoned you before he reached the city. You had said that you would help him; and I knew it was a lie. But what could I do? I tried to warn him. But he wouldn't listen. He thought that perhaps, after all these years, I might have reason to keep you two apart. He wouldn't listen to me. He would tell me nothing of his plans, except that you were going to help him…"

"You're insane," Mirche managed to say.

"Shut up, fool," sighed Owen. "You can't change the pattern."

"…So I followed you, Dan—in the car you gave me, and with the chauffeur you supplied from your own crooked gang." She laughed again, with the same bitterness. "He hates you as much as I do—but he's afraid of you, for he knows how dangerous you can be… I followed you from the time you left here Saturday afternoon. I knew you wouldn't let Benny come to you—in spite of your vicious cruelty, you're a coward. And I followed you uptown, and saw you go to Tony's place… Too bad Rosa didn't squint in her crystal and warn you!… And then I knew what a dirty deal you planned for Benny. But I didn't think you had the guts to do it as you did. I thought that Benny was to die only when you yourself were safely back here. How could I tell that you had chosen Tony's cigarettes for the job? I thought I could still warn Benny before it was too late—I thought I could still save him. So I followed you. I saw you pick him up from where he was hiding, far up in the park; I saw you drive north through Riverdale; I saw you stop at a lonely spot around a bend, where you thought no one could see you. And then I saw you place his body quickly beside the road and drive off."

She swept us with a burning glance.

"Oh, I'm not lying!" she cried. "Nothing matters any more—except the punishment of this creature."

Mirche seemed paralyzed, unable to speak. Owen, still with his cynical detached smile, had not moved.

"Please continue, Miss Del Marr," Vance requested.

"I took Benny's body into my own car, and I brought him back here when I knew Mirche would be upstairs. I came into the driveway, as I always do, and stopped close to the side door at the end of that passage." She pointed toward the rear of the room. "No one could see from the street—not with the car door open. And the ivy helped, too. Then I went inside to make sure no one was in the hall beyond, and I gave the signal. My driver carried poor Benny in here, as I had instructed him, through that secret door; and placed him in the cabinet where I keep the café records locked. Yes! I brought Benny back and placed him at the very feet of his murderer!... You didn't know, did you, Owl, that a dead man was in that cabinet when you sat here talking with me that night?"

"What of it?" There was no change in Owen's expression.

"And when you went out, Owl, I moved Benny to the desk and telephoned the police."

I now realized that Vance had deliberately provoked the woman's frantic outburst. As she was speaking he had made a sign to the Sergeant; and Heath and Hennessey had surreptitiously closed in on Mirche, so that they now stood guard on either side of him.

"But how, Miss Del Marr," asked Vance, "does your story account for the fact that the jonquille-scented cigarette case was found in Pellinzi's pocket?"

"Fear!—the conscience of this animal," she retorted, pointing defiantly at Mirche. "When he saw what he thought was Allen's body, his muddled, frightened brain remembered that in his own pocket was that man's cigarette case; and as he knelt beside the body, I saw him slip the case into the dead man's coat. The impulsive act of a coward, by which he meant to rid himself of all association with what he thought a *second* death. He shrank from any possible connection with *another* dead man."

"A reasonable version," murmured Vance. "Yes. A rather subtle analysis... And you were content to let the truth regarding the dead man emerge through natural channels?"

"Yes! After I informed the police of Allen's address, I knew they'd find out the truth sooner or later. And in the meantime this creature would worry and suffer—and I'd have plenty of ways of torturing him."

"The ethics of woman..." Owen began; then lapsed into silence.

"Have you anything to say before we arrest you, Mirche?" Vance's tone was low, but it cut like a lash.

Mirche stared hideously, and his flabby figure seemed to shrink. Suddenly, however, he drew himself up, and shook a quivering finger at Owen. His veins stood out like cords.

Owen made a small contemptuous noise.

"Your blood pressure, fool," he scoffed. "Don't cheat the gibbet."

I doubt if Mirche heard the biting words. Vituperation and profanity poured from him. His wrath seemed to surpass all human bounds. His venom left him a mere automaton—insensate, contorted, repulsive.

"You think I'll take the rap for you—without a word! I have knuckled under too long already to your bidding. I carried out your dirty schemes for you. I've shut my mouth whenever they tried to twist from me the filthy truth about you. I may go to the chair, Owl—but not alone! I'll take you and your poisoned, hypnotic brain along with me!"

He flashed a look at Vance, and pointed anew at Owen.

"There's the twisted mind behind it all!... I warned him of the Buzzard's arrival, and he sent me for the cigarettes. He told me what I must do. I was afraid to refuse—I was in his power..."

Owen looked at the man with calm derision: he was still aloof and scornful. The play was drawing to a close, and his contemptuous boredom had not abated.

"You're an unclean spectacle, Dan." His lips barely moved.

"You think I haven't prepared myself against this moment? *You* are the fool—not *me*. I've kept every record—names, dates, places—all! For years I've kept them. I've hidden them where no one can find them. But *I* know where to find them! And the world will know—"

Those were the last words Mirche ever spoke.

There was a shot. A small black hole appeared on Mirche's forehead between the eyes. Blood trickled from it. The man fell forward over the desk.

Heath and the two officers, their automatics drawn, started swiftly across the room to the passive Owen who sat without moving, one hand lying limply in his lap, holding a smoking revolver.

But Vance quickly intervened. His back to the silent figure in the chair, he faced Heath with a commanding gesture. Leisurely he turned, and extended his hand. Owen glanced up at him; then, as if with instinctive courtesy, he turned the revolver round and held it out with meek indifference. Vance tossed the weapon into an empty chair and, looking down again at the man, waited.

Owen's eyes were half closed and dreamy. He no longer seemed to be aware of his surroundings or of the sprawled body of Mirche whom he had just killed. Finally he spoke, his voice seeming to come from far off.

"That would have meant ripples."

Vance nodded.

"Yes. Cleanliness of spirit... But now there's the trial, and the chair, and the scandal—indelibly written..."

A shudder shook Owen's slight frame. His voice rose to a shrill cry.

"But how can one escape the finite—how cut through the shadow—*clean*?"

Vance took out his cigarette case and held it for a moment in his hand; but he did not open it.

"Would you care to smoke, Mr. Owen?" he asked.

The man's eyes contracted. Vance dropped his cigarette case back into his pocket.

"Yes..." Owen breathed at length. "I believe I *shall* have a cigarette." He reached into an inner pocket and drew forth a small Florentine-leather case...

"See here, Vance!" snapped Markham. "This is no longer *your* affair. A murder has been committed before my eyes, and I myself order this man's arrest."

"Quite," Vance drawled. "But I fear you are too late."

Even as he spoke, Owen slumped deeper in his chair; the cigarette he had lighted slipped from his lips and fell to the floor. Vance quickly crushed it with his foot.

Owen's head fell forward on his breast—the muscles of his neck had suddenly relaxed.

CHAPTER TWENTY

Happy Landing
(Wednesday, May 22; 10:30 a.m.)

THE FOLLOWING MORNING Vance was sitting in the District Attorney's office, talking with Markham. Heath had been there earlier with his report of the arrest of the Tofanas. Sufficient evidence had been unearthed in the cellar of their house to convict them both—or so the Sergeant hoped.

Dixie Del Marr had also called, at Markham's request, to supply such details as were needed for the official records. As there was no question of pressing charges against her for the part she had played in Mirche's affairs, she was comparatively content when she left us.

"Really, y' know, Markham," Vance remarked, "in view of the woman's primitive infatuation for Benny Pellinzi, her conduct, as we know it, is quite understandable—and forgivable... As for Mirche, his end was far better than he deserved... And Owen! A diseased maniac. Fortunate for the world he chose so expeditious a way of making his exit! He knew he was dying; and the stalking dread of a vengeful hereafter inspired his act... We may well be content to call the whole matter closed. And, after all, I did give the lunatic a vague promise to guard his aftermath so there should be no 'ripples,' as he put it, to follow him."

Vance laughed dismally.

"What does it really matter? A minor gangster is found dead—a quite commonplace event; a major gangster is shot— also an ordin'ry episode; and the guiding light of a criminal band turns *felo de se*—well, perhaps a rare occurrence, but certainly not important... And anyway, the year's at the spring; the lark's on the wing; the snail's on the thorn—I say! how about some *escargots Bordelaise* later?"

As he spoke, the buzzer sounded, and a voice announced the presence of Mr. Amos Doolson in the outer office.

Markham looked at Vance.

"I suppose it's about that preposterous reward. But I can't see the man now—"

Vance stood up quickly.

"Keep him waiting, Markham! An idea smites me!"

Then he went to the telephone and spoke to the In-O-Scent Corporation. When he hung up the receiver he smiled at Markham. "Gracie Allen and George Burns will be here in fifteen minutes." He chuckled with genuine delight. If anyone deserves that reward, it's the dryad. And I'm going to see that she gets it."

"Are you out of your mind!" exclaimed Markham in surprise.

"No—oh, no. Quite sane, don't y' know. And—though you may doubt it—I'm passionately devoted to justice."

Miss Allen, with Mr. Burns, arrived shortly thereafter.

"Oh, what a *terrible* place!" she said. "I'm glad *I* don't have to live here, Mr. Markham." She turned troubled eyes on

Vance. "Have I *got* to go on with my detecting? I'd *much* rather work at the factory—now that George is back, and everything."

"No, my dear," said Vance kindly. "You have already done ample. And the results you have achieved have been superb. In fact, I wanted you to come here this morning merely to receive your reward. A reward of five thousand dollars was offered to the person who would solve the murder of that man in the *Domdaniel*. It was Mr. Doolson who made the offer; and he's waiting in the other room now."

"Oh!" For once the girl was too puzzled and stunned to speak.

When Doolson was ushered in he took one amazed look at his two employees and went direct to Markham's desk.

"I want to withdraw that reward immediately, sir," he said. "Burns came back to work this morning in excellent spirits, and therefore there is no necessity—"

Markham, who had readily adjusted himself to Vance's jocular but equitable view of the situation, spoke in his most judicial manner.

"I regret extremely, Mr. Doolson, that such a withdrawal is entirely out of the question. The case was completed and shelved yesterday afternoon—well within the time limit you stipulated. I have no alternative but to pay that money to the person who earned it."

The man's gorge rose and he spluttered.

"But—!" he began to expostulate.

"We're frightfully sorry, and all that, Mr. Doolson," Vance cut in dulcetly. "But I am sure you will be quite reconciled to your impulsive generosity when I inform you that the recipient is to be Miss Gracie Allen."

"*What!*" Doolson burst forth apoplectically. "What has Miss Allen to do with it? Preposterous!"

"No," replied Vance. "Simple statement of fact. Miss Allen had everything to do with the solution of the case. It was she who supplied every important clue... And, after all, you did get back the services of your Mr. Burns today."

"I won't do it!" shouted the man. "It's chicanery! A farce! You can't legally hold me to it!"

"On the contrary, Mr. Doolson," said Markham, "I am forced to regard the money as the property of the young lady. The very wording of the reward—dictated here by yourself— would not leave you a leg to stand on if you decided to make a legal issue of it."

Doolson's jaw sagged.

"Oh, Mr. Doolson!" exclaimed Gracie Allen. "That's such a *lovely* reward! And did you *really* do it to get George back to work for the big rush? I never thought of that. But you *do* need him terribly, don't you?... And oh, that gives me another idea. You ought to raise George's salary."

"I'll be damned if I will!" For a moment I thought Doolson was on the verge of a stroke.

"But just suppose, Mr. Doolson," Miss Allen went on, "if George got worried again and couldn't do his work! What *would* become of the business?"

The man took hold of himself and studied Burns darkly and thoughtfully for several moments.

"You know, Burns," he said almost placatingly, "I've been thinking for some time that you deserved a raise. You've been most loyal and valuable to the corporation. You come back to your laboratory at once—and we can discuss the matter amicably." Then he turned and shook his finger wrathfully at the girl. "And *you*, young woman. *You're* fired!"

"Oh, that's all right, Mr. Doolson," the girl returned with smiling nonchalance. "I bet the raise you give George will make his salary as much as his and mine put together now—if you know what I mean."

"Who gives a damn what you mean!" And Doolson stalked angrily from the room.

"I believe," said Vance musingly, "that the next remark should come from Mr. Burns himself." And he smiled at the young man significantly.

Burns, though obviously astonished by the proceedings of the past half-hour, was nevertheless sufficiently clear-headed to understand the import of Vance's words. Grasping the suggestion offered, he walked resolutely to the girl.

"How about that proposition I made to you the morning I was arrested?" Our presence, far from embarrassing him, had given him courage.

"Why, what proposition?" the girl asked archly.

"You know what I mean!" His tone was gruff and determined. "How about you and me getting married?"

The girl fell back into a chair, laughing musically.

"Oh, George! Was *that* what you were trying to say!"

There is little more that need be told regarding what Vance has always insisted on calling the Gracie Allen murder case.

The *Domdaniel*, as everyone knows, has long been closed, and a few years ago it was replaced by a modern commercial structure. Tony and Rosa Tofana found it expedient to confess, and are now serving time in prison. I do not know what became of Dixie Del Marr. She probably took a new name and left this part of the country, to live quietly far from the scenes of her former triumphs and tragedies.

Gracie Allen and George Burns were married shortly after that unexpected and amusing proposal in Markham's office.

One Saturday afternoon, months later, Vance and I met them strolling down Fifth Avenue. They seemed inordinately happy, and the girl was chatting animatedly, as usual.

We stopped for a few minutes to speak with them. We learned that Burns had been made a junior officer in the In-O-Scent Corporation; and, much to Vance's delight, the fact came out that Miss Allen had, for sentimental reasons, presented his card to Mr. Lyons of Chareau and Lyons, when selecting her wedding dress.

As we walked with them a short distance, Burns, in the midst of a sentence, suddenly stopped, and I noticed that his nostrils dilated slightly as he leaned close to Vance.

"Farina's original formula of *Eau de Cologne!*"

Vance laughed.

"Yes. I always bring back a supply from Europe... Which reminds me: this morning I saw in a French magazine the name of a perfume, which, after the indispensable work Mrs. Burns did on our case, you might most appropriately give to the delightful citron-scented mixture you made for her. It was called *La Femme Triomphante.*"

Burns grinned proudly.

"I guess Gracie did help you a lot, Mr. Vance."

The girl looked from one to the other with a puzzled frown, and then laughed shyly.

"I don't get it."

We hope you loved *The Gracie Allen Murder Case.*

If Philo Vance is your cup of tea, you may also like Elizabeth Daly's Henry Gamadge series. Gamadge is a classic gentleman sleuth of the Golden Age—an expert in rare books and documents consulting on high-society crimes. He's less snooty than Vance but just as intelligent and refined, and Daly's writing is a treat. She was, notably, Agatha Christie's favorite mystery author. We've included the first few chapters of *Unexpected Night* (Henry Gamadge #1) to give you a taste—enjoy!

UNEXPECTED NIGHT

CHAPTER ONE

A Pale Young Man

PINE TRUNKS IN a double row started out of the mist as the headlights caught them, opened to receive the car, passed like an endless screen, and vanished. The girl on the back seat withdrew her head from the open window.

"We'll never get there at this rate," she said. "We're crawling."

The older woman sat far back in her corner, a figure of exhausted elegance. She said, keeping her voice low: "In this fog, I don't think it would be safe to hurry."

"I should think it would be safer than keeping him up all night."

"We'll see what Hugh thinks."

But the speaker did not move immediately. She looked too tired to move. Her face, under the short veil and the close black hat, showed white in the dimness, of the same whiteness as the small pearls in her ears. Presently she leaned forward, her high-collared woollen coat falling softly away and showing the dark silk dress beneath. She put a hand in a white glove on the back of the driver's seat.

"Can we go a little faster, Hugh?" she asked. "It's so late."

"It's this fog."

"I think it's only what they call a sea turn, up here; it will blow over before morning."

"Scares me to death. I don't know the road, and we don't want any bumps."

"Is he all right?" She peered anxiously at what looked like a heap of rugs beside the driver—a heap surmounted by a Panama hat. It stirred, and she asked: "Are you all right, Amby?"

A voice replied, drowsily: "All right. Been having a nap." It added, rather crossly: "Don't be feeble, Hugh. Step on it."

The car picked up speed.

"I'm sorry if I waked you, dear." The woman's voice was calm and cheerful, but her gloved hand gripped the edge of the seat in front. "Would you like another little drink of brandy?"

"No, thanks, Aunt El. Don't worry about me." The words were polite, but the tone was dry. "I'll make it."

She sat back, resting her head, trimly encased in the small hat, against the back of her seat. The young man called Hugh kept his eyes on the road, but he nudged the other with an elbow, and slightly shook his head. A face, which had until now been almost entirely hidden between the turned-down hat brim and the turned-up collar of a heavy topcoat, looked upwards and caught the light. It had fine dark eyes, but in all other respects it resembled a death mask that had been tinted blue, even to the lips. It spoke, with amiable irony:

"Calm yourself; I'll be good."

"You'd better be, old boy."

"I get so sick of all the fussing."

"You ought to be grateful for it."

"This 'bring 'em back alive' business gets on my nerves."

"It gets on my nerves when you talk that rot. Insulting people that care for you!"

"Invalids always get that way. Didn't you know?"

"You've been spoiled. If you were well, I'd take it out of you. You think you can say anything."

"That's because I can't do anything. It gets on my nerves."

"You and your nerves. If you had any nerves, you wouldn't be planning this crazy trip, to-morrow."

"I'm going, if it's the last thing I do."

"I ought to tell your aunt about it."

"She couldn't stop me. I'll be of age—don't forget that."

"I'm not likely to forget it; you don't talk about anything else." The young man paused, and then said, slowly: "You know I don't run people down, as a rule; but if Atwood had any decency, he wouldn't let you try it."

"He's all right. He doesn't keep on lecturing me, anyway."

"What's a tutor for?"

"You won't be a tutor much longer."

"Don't remind me of it. I'm trying to get in a few last licks, to-night."

The boy hesitated, and then said persuasively: "You know I've asked you again and again to come up there with me."

"Go barnstorming with you in that summer theatre? Certainly not. I haven't taken leave of my senses."

"There's nothing crazy about a summer theatre."

"There is for you. Look here, Amby; why not let me drive on straight to the hotel? It's getting on to midnight. You must be pretty well done up after that bad turn you had to-day, and your aunt and sister are half dead."

"I'm always having bad turns; one, more or less, makes no difference to me. Fred's expecting us."

"I can telephone down from the hotel, and say you didn't feel up to it."

"No. I want to see him."

"And the doctor says you mustn't be thwarted. How you trade on that, young fellow!"

The pale young man, hunched to the ears in his topcoat, chuckled. His sister spoke from the back seat, after drawing her head in at the car window: "That Ford hasn't passed us yet."

"What Ford?" The driver glanced back.

"It's been following us for miles."

The pale young man turned to look at her face, which showed, a white blur, in the car's dark interior. Then he, also, craned out of his window. When he drew his head in, he said cheerfully: "You're crazy. Here she comes, now."

A horn sounded, and the small car passed them. Its driver, a small man in a sou'wester much too big for him, flashed by and vanished in the mist ahead. The boy laughed, teasingly. "No holdups to-night," he said. "Poor old Alma. No excitement."

"We're almost there." His aunt leaned forward to look out of the car. "Yes, just a minute or two more. Turn right, Hugh, and then straight along the shore road. The Barclay cottage is the second on the left."

The screen of trees had rolled up at last. They were in the open, rumbling across a wooden bridge; a salt smell came from the marshes on either hand, but the fog closed in now like a barrage. The car slowed down.

"This is bad," said the driver.

"Only a minute more, Hugh. The second cottage on the left."

The Barclay cottage, a gabled relic of the eighties, was situated rather bleakly on the outskirts of a small summer resort called Ford's Beach. Its only small, dry front yard, a sandy road, and a low rampart of rock were all that separated it from the ocean. It was also rather bleak within. Its combination lobby, living and dining room—walled, ceiled and floored with native pine—was made cheerful by a log fire, and a faded Navajo blanket on a couch in one corner; there was no other brightness or colour, no pictures, no knick-knacks, and no flowers.

Four persons sat around a bridge table, in the glare of a droplight: Colonel and Mrs. Barclay, their son, Lieutenant Frederic Barclay, and a guest from the hotel, a Mr. Henry Gamadge. The time was twenty minutes to twelve o'clock, and the date was Sunday night, June 25, 1939.

The three men were adding up scores; Mrs. Barclay was digging small change out of the cavernous recesses of a large knitting bag. She looked, and was, an old campaigner. As an Army wife she had learned to travel light, and had forever lost the habit of collecting bric-a-brac, or of regarding her home as anything more permanent than officer's quarters in a camp or barracks. Mrs. Barclay liked to think that she was a cosmopolitan, and had somehow acquired the notion that this involved wearing a curled fringe or bang, and piling the rest of her light hair high on the top of her head. She also felt obliged to dress formally in the evening, no matter what the circumstances; grudging exception being made in the case of picnics and dining-cars. On this occasion she wore a limp, flowered costume, cut very low; a fluttering chiffon scarf; and several strings of Venetian glass beads.

She was tall, thin, and very strong. Her game of golf was formidable, but she ruined her score on the approaches and the greens. She drove the family car much as she had once ridden a horse—sitting very straight, and bumping very much.

Colonel Barclay was a short, round man with a sunburned face and a clipped grey moustache. He was immaculate, if a little shabby, in yellowing white flannel trousers and a tight, blue serge coat. His son, Lieutenant Frederic Barclay, was also immaculate, and also shabby; but the resemblance between them went no farther. Lieutenant Barclay, Field Artillery, stationed in the South, and now spending his leave (for economy's sake) with his parents, was a tall, broad-shouldered and extremely handsome young man. He had long, dark, sleepy-looking eyes, smooth, dark hair, and a clear skin, slightly tanned. He moved slowly and deliberately, without effort; and he looked presentable in anything.

Mr. Henry Gamadge, on the other hand, wore clothes of excellent material and cut; but he contrived, by sitting and walking in a careless and lopsided manner, to look presentable in nothing. He screwed his grey tweeds out of shape before he had worn them a week, he screwed his mouth to one side when he smiled, and he screwed his eyes up when he pondered. His eyes were greyish green, his features blunt, and his hair mouse-coloured. People as a rule considered him a well-mannered, restful kind of young man; but if somebody happened to say something unusually outrageous or inane, he was wont to gaze upon the speaker in a wondering and somewhat disconcerting manner.

He said now, writing something on his score pad, and drawing a circle around it, "It's getting a little late. Shall we go on, or shall we have the return rubber another night? Perhaps you'll play with me to-morrow, at the Ocean House."

"Going on midnight." The colonel looked up at his watch. "We'll have to wait up," he grumbled, "but we'll let you off, if you like."

"I have an early golf match to-morrow, or I wouldn't suggest stopping. I'm afraid I'm the big winner."

Mrs. Barclay fished a heap of small change out of her knitting bag. "I don't feel like any more bridge to-night," she said. "Let me see, Mr. Gamadge. At a twentieth of a cent, I must owe you a dollar."

"That's right, Mrs. Barclay; but it can stand over."

"No, indeed. My father always said, 'Never get up from the bridge table owing money.' I should be the winner, really."

"Yes. Hard luck."

"I suppose it was mad to redouble the spades, but I was counting on Freddy. He is such a good holder, usually. I was counting on him."

"Lots of psychology in family bridge." Her son subdued a yawn. "How far am I down, Gamadge?"

"You're up thirty cents. Thirty cents to your offspring, Colonel."

"Come across, Dad."

Colonel Barclay heaved himself sidewise in his chair, got two dimes and two nickels out of his trouser pocket, and shoved them over the khaki bridge-table cover towards his son. "You'll be wanting to get to bed, Gamadge," he said, "if you have a nine o'clock golf match."

"I have, sir; with old Mr. Macpherson from Montreal."

"But you must wait and have a nightcap with us. I was sure the Cowdens would be here long before this."

"They couldn't make it much earlier than twelve, leaving Portsmouth at about ten," said young Barclay. "Sanderson telephoned from there, you know. He said he was going to drive slowly."

"Eleanor must be mad," complained Mrs. Barclay. "Ridiculous to stop here. Not that it isn't very sweet of your cousin to want to see you, Freddy. Still, to-morrow would do."

"'To-morrow' isn't a date he can be sure of keeping, you know, Mum."

"My dear child! And don't you give him his present to-night, whatever you do. It's very unlucky to give birthday presents before the day."

"He'll think he's very unlucky to get this one, whenever he gets it."

"Now, Freddy; a lovely case, for his medicated cigarettes! The prettiest one in the gift shop."

"He has one, and it came from Bond Street, I think. Or Cartier's."

"This will be just the thing for ordinary use. It's such a sad story, Mr. Gamadge; really a tragedy."

"Your nephew is so very seriously ill?"

"Incurably so. It's his heart. He had rheumatic fever while he was quite a child, and the aftereffects were very serious. He cannot live long. He has these attacks more and more often; he had one to-night, just before they reached Portsmouth. But he insisted on coming along to-night."

"Curious that his people should allow it," said Gamadge.

"They don't cross him," said the Colonel. "They do as he pleases. He should have been brought up to obey orders."

"Now, Father, it's easy to say that, but it has been a dreadful problem for poor Eleanor; my sister-in-law, Mr. Gamadge—she's his guardian; his parents are dead. My brother was appointed guardian to both the children, and then he died, and now Eleanor looks after them."

"Two children, are there?"

"Oh, yes. Brother and sister."

"Alma doesn't count—yet," said young Barclay, smiling a little.

"Of course she counts, Freddy! What a thing to say!"

"You'll have to tell Gamadge all about it, Mum; he looks interested."

Gamadge was glad that he had given that impression. He said: "There's a story, is there?"

"A very interesting story, Mr. Gamadge. A very peculiar story. My nephew Amberley will be twenty-one years old to-morrow, and he will come into nearly a million dollars."

"Whew!"

"If he lives," said young Barclay. He consulted his watch, and added: "Sixty-eight minutes to go. I should say he'd make it."

"Freddy!"

"Well, Mum, we're all pretty well used to the situation by this time. Matter of fact, he may live for years."

"It *is* an interesting situation, though," said Gamadge. "May I ask what would have happened to the million if he hadn't lived?"

"That's what makes it so interesting," said young Barclay, in a dry tone. "Every cent of it would go to some French connections that none of us has ever laid eyes on."

An ancient grievance was smouldering in Mrs. Barclay's eye. She said crossly: "I still think that will could have been broken. I said at the time that it could have been broken. I begged and implored Mr. Ormville—that's our lawyer, Mr. Gamadge—I begged him—"

The Colonel spoke rather impatiently: "Ormville knows what can and can't be done, Lulu. The will was all right."

"It was iniquitous! My oldest sister, Mr. Gamadge, was eccentric; I still think that she had become irresponsible."

"Mum was ready and willing to shoot her into a lunatic asylum, weren't you, poor old Mum?" laughed Fred Barclay.

"I certainly should have done something about it if I had known; but we didn't know, unfortunately, Mr. Gamadge... until she died. You see, she had married a Frenchman, and she had lived in France for years. She had become very peculiar even before she died. She didn't care for any of us any more— her own relations!—except my brother, Amberley's father. He took the child over there to see her, and she immediately took a fancy to the child. It amounted to infatuation."

"And you took this child over to see her, and she took anything but a fancy to me," laughed Fred Barclay.

Mrs. Barclay ignored him. "Amberley has stayed with her several times. She took him to specialists. She gave him a huge allowance. And when she died, she left a will leaving him all her money—if he should live to be twenty-one years old. If he didn't, it was to go to her husband's French relations."

"I see," said Gamadge. "It was her husband's money, was it?"

"Oh, yes; he was a very rich man. Some of them are, you know—they make it in Indo-China, or somewhere. I thought him very vulgar."

"Not at all," growled the Colonel. "Good sort of fellow."

"You should see his relations, Harrison! You never met them, but I did. Freddy is wrong when he says none of us has ever laid eyes on them. I did, years ago."

"Mother has met everybody, at one time or another," said young Barclay, shuffling the cards.

"But they weren't anybody, Fred. Well, that's how it is, Mr. Gamadge. Can you imagine the strain it has all been for poor Eleanor Cowden, my sister-in-law?"

Fred Barclay burst out laughing. "You're a caution, Mum. No wonder the lot of you have turned poor old Amby into a cynic."

"You know perfectly what I mean, dear, and it is very wrong of you to take that attitude. We are all devoted to Amberley, Mr. Gamadge. His illness has been a great anxiety to us all. Of course it has warped him a little; it would be a miracle if it hadn't. But everybody tells me that Mr. Sanderson—that's his tutor, Mr. Gamadge—has done wonders for the child's morale."

"He plays the deuce with mine, though." Young Barclay tilted his chair back against the wall. "Makes me tired. 'Doesn't your sister need a change of air after her cold? Have some consideration for your dear aunt.' That sort of thing."

"Mr. Sanderson is not at all like that, Freddy. If it were not for him, Amberley would be spoiled—utterly spoiled. He was beginning to think of nothing and nobody but himself. I was surprised and delighted when you told me about his making that will."

"Another source of strain," said Fred Barclay, glancing at Gamadge. "He can't make a will until tomorrow, of course; but he's got one all written out and ready to sign."

"Three witnesses are required in this state, dear; don't forget that," begged Mrs. Barclay.

"Perhaps Gamadge will oblige; and you and Dad. The rest of the family are beneficiaries," said her son. "There's only one shadow to mar the rosy prospect, Mum; he's sure to have left a slice—and a big one—to Arthur Atwood."

"Oh, dear!" sighed Mrs. Barclay.

The Colonel drummed on the table. "I don't want to hear a word more about this," he said, angrily. "It's repulsive."

"But, dear," protested his wife, "we all know that Arthur Atwood is perfectly horrible."

"Arthur Atwood," explained Fred Barclay, for Gamadge's benefit, "is the son of Mother's next most eccentric sister. So there you have the whole family; and we might as well include poor old Alma, insignificant as she seems, because if Amberley dies intestate she'll get all his money; unless he manages to give it away first. I shouldn't be surprised if he did. He's dying to get his hands on the principal. You can understand that he hasn't been able to raise a cent on his expectations."

"Of course not. Too bad a life," said Gamadge.

"No insurance, no borrowing, no anything. He's had this big allowance, though, and we've all been battening on it."

"Generous with it, is he?"

"In his own way."

"Haven't his aunt and his sister any money of their own?"

"Not much—have they, Dad?"

"None of us has had much since 1929." The Colonel got up. "I believe I hear the car."

Mrs. Barclay arose, and hastily followed her husband out on the porch. Young Barclay strolled after them. The open door let in a gush of damp air. Gamadge, whose interest in the arrivals had been considerably aroused, listened to the slamming of car doors, the chorus of greeting, the noise of many footsteps on gravel and then on wood. A crowd surged into the room.

"You must all be chilled to the bone. Come in, come in and get warm," trumpeted the Colonel. "Hot or cold drinks— all ready." He disappeared into the pantry.

Mrs. Barclay advanced, her arm in that of a tall, slender figure, beautifully dressed; her son followed more slowly, his arm about the shoulders of a smaller, slighter young man, beside whom a light-haired youth in a raincoat hovered anxiously. A dark girl brought up the rear of the procession. She stood for a moment or two in the doorway, and then closed the door and went over to a window. As she leaned there, looking out at the opaque curtain of mist beyond, Gamadge thought that she seemed neglected, unhappy and forlorn. She was rather casually dressed in a dark-blue flannel skirt, a rose-coloured blouse, and a leather coat. She wore no hat. Her dark hair, cut very short, lay as smoothly as a cap on her small head.

Young Barclay and the man in the raincoat had shep-herded their charge to the fire, and were relieving him of his heavy tweed ulster, his white silk scarf, and his fine Ecuadorian Panama. Mrs. Barclay seized Gamadge's arm.

"Mr. Gamadge, I should like to introduce you to my sister-in-law, Mrs. Cowden. Eleanor, this is Mr. Gamadge, a friend of Fred's."

"How do you do?" said Mrs. Cowden, smiling. Gamadge saw that Mrs. Barclay had been right—Mrs. Cowden could smile and be civil, but she was indeed suffering from strain.

"How do you do?" he said. "You must be tired."

"We all are, a little."

"And this," said Mrs. Barclay, still gripping Gamadge's arm, and drawing him towards the fire, "this is my nephew. Dear Amberley. And Mr. Sanderson, who takes such good care of him."

The sudden modulation of her tone from affection to condescension might well have cut an oversensitive person like a knife; but Mr. Sanderson seemed to be philosophical; his thin, good-looking face registered nothing but polite good humour. He had turned from his charge, and was steering in the direction of Miss Cowden and the window. Mrs. Barclay said:

"Oh—there is dear Alma. I want you to meet Alma, Mr. Gamadge. I didn't see you, dear. This is Mr. Gamadge."

Alma Cowden nodded.

"Are you comfortable, Amby? Getting warm?" Mrs. Barclay dropped Gamadge's arm, and returned to the fireplace. "Fred, where is Amby's cocoa?"

Fred went into the pantry, and Gamadge went up to the young man who stood in front of the hearth. He had been prepared for symptoms of serious illness, but nothing could have prepared him for the skim-milk translucence of the face that smiled up at him. Its dark eyes looked like onyx against that pallor.

"Are you an old-timer here, Mr. Gamadge?" he asked.

"I think I may say so. I've been coming every summer for years."

"This is my first trip. Have you ever been up to a place called Seal Cove?"

"I've missed that."

"They tell me it's quite a short trip—just a few miles beyond Oakport. I have a cousin up there, this summer; he's helping to run a summer theatre."

"Interesting job."

"It opens to-morrow night. I wouldn't miss it for anything. Do you go to summer theatres much?"

"Well, to tell you the truth, not unless somebody hauls me. I must admit I like winter ones best."

The boy laughed, gaily. "This one is going to be better than most. They've got a manager that used to be with the Abbey Theatre—you know. I've met him. He's crazy about the Irish drama. Do you like the Irish drama, Mr. Gamadge?"

"Hang it all," said Gamadge, "I seem to be a complete blight, this evening. I *don't* care so very much about it, to be perfectly frank; but then, I haven't read all of it, or seen much of it. Perhaps I haven't given it a chance."

"Why don't you come up and try it at Seal Cove?" Young Cowden's face assumed a gleeful and impish expression. "I have an interest in drumming up audiences, you know. I'm... "

He had pulled off a pair of thick chamois gloves, and was twisting them into a rope. As his cousin appeared with a tray, he shoved them into a pocket, and produced a truly magnificent cigarette case. It was thin, made of platinum, and initialled in gold. "I won't offer you a cigarette," he said; "I only smoke those awful things without any tobacco in them."

"Without any nicotine, you mean, you young ass." Fred Barclay put the tray down on a stand, and poured out a cup. "Have some of this stuff, Alma?"

Alma Cowden, followed by Sanderson, came up to them.

"Don't look so cross," said her brother.

"I'm not cross."

"Cross as a bear all day. Isn't that so, Hugh?"

"Stop badgering your sister, and give me one of those gaspers of yours. I rather like them."

"I don't." Miss Cowden, ignoring young Barclay's prof-fered case, fished a crumpled package of cigarettes from her pocket. Sanderson gave her a light. He, too, was a little thread-bare; his Harris tweeds had seen better days. In fact, of all the men in the room, the sick boy alone looked, and unconsciously behaved, like a rich man. "The heir," Gamadge reflected, "and his poor relations. It leaps to the eye."

Colonel Barclay, tray in hand, pushed at the swing door with his foot. Gamadge went over, relieved him of his burden, and set it on the bridge table. This had been drawn up beside the couch where Mrs. Barclay sat in deep conversation with her sister-in-law.

"Family reunion," thought Gamadge. "I ought to go. A short drink, and I'm off." He helped the colonel to mix high-balls, while the two ladies chatted, practically in his ear:

"Of course it is dreadful to have to let him do these things, Lulu; but he must be kept happy."

"I should have thought, though, that if this attack at Portsmouth was so serious—"

"All his attacks are serious. We got a room for him, and Hugh Sanderson got him to bed; but he would get up and come on to-night. All he can think of is this wretched summer theatre. It opens tomorrow night, and he is determined to be on hand."

"Because those Atwoods are there!"

"And a little girl called Baker. He adores it all."

"He never would have got into it if it hadn't been for the Atwoods."

"I tried my best to break up the intimacy; he's been cross with me ever since. But that studio of theirs in New York was so bad for him—the smoke, and the crowds, and the excitement. Poor child, he hasn't had much fun, of course. You don't know what a strain it's all been, these last years. Oh, thank you, Mr. Gamadge. That looks just right."

She took the glass from him, and sat back against the cushions to enjoy it. Gamadge, mixing Mrs. Barclay's drink, glanced at her with admiration. Fine bones, fine skin, level eyebrows over hazel eyes, beautiful figure, beautiful, simple clothes. She must be in her late forties, but with that physique she would always be good-looking. The rippling brown hair that showed under one side of her small hat had no grey in it, but he would swear it wasn't dyed. Just one of those lucky people that couldn't grow old.

Colonel Barclay came up, and drew a chair to Mrs. Cowden's side. "Sit down, Gamadge," he said, patting the back of another one.

"No, thank you, Colonel. I'll just swallow this, and then I must go."

"Can we give you a lift to the hotel?" asked Mrs. Cowden. "If you don't mind a lot of things falling all over your feet, there's plenty of room."

"Thank you very much, I have my small bus."

He finished his whisky, shook hands with her and with his host and hostess, and crossed the room. Miss Cowden had again retired to the window, and Mr. Sanderson had again joined her there. Lieutenant Barclay was handing a paper to Amberley Cowden, who said, as he shoved it into a pocket: "What do you think?"

"Fine. But you'll live to bury the lot of us."

"Don't be silly."

"Too bad Aunt El is in such a deuce of a hurry; you could have stayed here till the zero hour, and got it off your mind." He turned, as Gamadge came up. "Going, old man? I was just telling young Amberley that the state of Maine requires three witnesses to a will."

"Uncle and Aunt Lu and Mr. Gamadge could have signed; that's so. Well, to-morrow will do. Can't you wait and go up with us, Mr. Gamadge?"

"I have a little car outside. Good night, Mr. Cowden."

"Next time you see me, I'll be twenty-one."

"That so?"

"Yes. Goes by standard time." He consulted his watch. "It's only ten past eleven, really." He shook hands with Gamadge, who went over to the pair by the window. This time they were both contemplating the curtain of mist. When he spoke, they turned. Sanderson shook hands, amiably; but she did not at first seem to remember who Gamadge was, or why he was there. Her short, smooth dark hair, brushed straight back from her forehead, gave her a melancholy, Pierrot look, and her dark eyes met his with a brooding gaze.

"Good night, Miss Cowden."

"Good night."

He went out, turning up his collar; found his way across the yard to the road; stood for a moment admiring the big Cowden car, and then climbed into the modest coupé behind it, and drove off through the mist.

CHAPTER TWO

Gamadge Minds His Own Business

FROM THE BARCLAY Cottage to the Ocean House drive the shore road rises gently, curving to the left. It then dips again, runs level for a couple of miles, and turns inland through pinewoods to Oakport Village. Gamadge would have said that he knew every bump of it; but to-night the fog had dropped a veil over the familiar and the real. It had muffled the sound of the tide that came booming in below the rocks on the right, so that the surf might have been half a mile away, instead of just across the beach. It had dimmed the lights of the cottages on the left, so that these were confused with the bathhouse and the beach shops, and Gamadge thought he had passed the boardwalk long before he had reached it. He nearly missed the turn to the hotel.

He backed, went up the rough drive, and followed it past the Ocean House down to the garage. Drawing up in front of

the sign that said: "Please Do Not Blow Your Horn," he called
Kimball, the night man.

"Don't bury my car behind the big one that's coming in,"
he begged.

"Lots of room, this early in the season," replied Kimball.

Gamadge walked up to the hotel, climbed the steps,
crossed the wide veranda, and opened one of the doors that
led into the lobby. These were usually wide, but to-night they
were closed against the fog. Sam, the night watchman, sat
behind the counter, his feet up, eating a banana.

"Hello, Mr. Gamadge," he said. "Nice night for a drive."

"Fine. I hope it blows over before morning."

"It'll blow over before that."

"Your party from New York is on the way. I just saw them
down at the Barclays'."

"I'm all ready for 'em."

"Don't stare when you see the boy. He startles you, for
a minute. He has heart trouble, you know, and it makes him
a queer colour."

"I heard he was sick. How about my takin' him up in the
elevator?"

"The what?"

"The freight elevator."

"Oh, that thing. I don't think they'd trust him on it. If
they had to have an elevator for him, they'd have written and
asked about one."

"Mrs. Cowden's been here before. She knows there ain't
any."

"Have Waldo call me at eight, will you? I have a golf
date."

"O.K." Sam made a note on a pad. Gamadge's eye
wandered to the mailboxes, and he stared, unpleasantly
affected by what he saw.

"Don't tell me there's a letter for me."

"Seems so. And a big one," replied Sam, taking it out of
its pigeonhole, and handing it across the counter.

"Oh, Lord. Proof. I'll be at it an hour."

"Can't it wait till to-morrow?"

"No, it can't. I have to get it into the box for the early collection."

He climbed the first flight of wide, shallow stairs, and then the second, steeper one that led to his room on the second floor. He was as yet alone on this corridor, which somehow conveyed an impression of the fact, as hotel corridors mysteriously do, even without the testimony of dark, closed transoms and a minimum of light. Nobody had bothered to close the glass door at the end; it gave on the spiral stairway, enclosing the shaft of the freight elevator, that did duty at the Ocean House for fire escape. Salt air, damp and fog-laden, met Gamadge as he turned towards his room.

Should he close the end door? He decided against it, opened his own, and switched on his light. He took his coat off, sat down, put his feet up on the only other chair, got out his fountain pen, and went to work.

At five minutes past one Sam looked up from his magazine, saw the darkness beyond the glass of the front doors change to grey, to cloudy opalescence, to yellow. He jumped up, came from behind the counter, and hurried across the lobby and out on the porch. The Cowden car was just coming to a stop at the foot of the veranda steps. He ran down and opened the rear door.

"Glad to have you back, Mrs. Cowden," he said. "How are you?"

"Why, it's Sam. Nice to see you again. I've brought my family with me, this summer. This is my niece."

"How are you, Miss Cowden?" Sam helped the elder lady out, and would have done the same for the other; but she jumped down without his assistance, and ran up the steps and into the hotel, her little dressing case in her hand. The blond young man in the raincoat who had been behind the wheel slipped out, came around the car, and opened the near front door. Sam, getting out luggage, watched from the corner of his eye while he helped a bundled figure to descend, decided that his own help was not needed, and after one glimpse of the livid face between hat-brim and coat collar, turned away. When the bags were out, he put his fingers to his mouth and gave a low, owl-like hoot, which brought a similar response from the garage.

"Don't bother." The young man in the raincoat paused in his slow ascent of the steps, his arm in that of his companion. "I can drive the car down."

"No trouble. Kimball ain't busy." Sam started on his first trip into the hotel with the luggage, thinking: "They're all tuck- ered out, and three of 'em's scared to death. The sick feller ain't. Acts like he was enjoying it."

The pale young man had, in fact, straightened, thrown back his shoulders, shaken off Sanderson's arm, and looked about him with a cheerful smile. Mrs. Cowden, bringing up the rear with Sam, murmured: "My nephew isn't well."

"I heard he wasn't."

"We were terribly frightened on the way up from the Barclays'. He had some cocoa there. I don't think it agreed with him."

"That's too bad."

"I thought we should never get him here."

"Want I should call a doctor?"

"No, he says he's all right. But he always says that. Oh, dear! What is he doing now?"

The pale young man had walked across to the desk, and was writing in the register.

"Come off it, Amby," protested Sanderson. "No need for that. Come on up to bed."

Sam put the luggage on the floor, and went behind the counter to officiate. The young man looked up at him, and then, above his head, at the clock on the wall. He gave Sam a roguish and elfin smile.

"That clock of yours right?" he asked.

"Set it by radio every day."

"Then I've been of age for eleven minutes. This is my birthday."

"Many hap—" began Sam.

"I don't know about that; but I can do as I please, now, and I want to register." He finished his task, and Sam, blotting it, read, upside down:

Mrs. Francis Cowden, New York City.
Miss Alma Cowden,   "   "   "
Amberley Cowden,   "   "   "
Hugh Sanderson,   "   "   "

"That right?"

"It's exactly right, Mr. Cowden."

"Any telephone message for me?"

Sam investigated in the rack, and said there was none.

"Funny. All right, Hugh. I'll go up, now. What's the hurry?"

Sanderson, who had been exchanging helpless glances with Mrs. Cowden, propelled the recalcitrant young man toward the stairs. Miss Cowden had been standing halfway up, her back turned to them all. Sam picked up three bags, and led the way to the first door.

"Right down here," he said, walking the length of the corridor, and stopping in front of a room just to the right of the fire-escape door. "Number 21—that's yours, Mrs. Cowden. Miss Cowden has 19, next door; bath between. Mr. Cowden is in 17, with bath. Mr. Sanderson is opposite, Number 20; single, no bath. That right?"

"That's right, thank you, Sam. Just bring the rest of the things up, and we'll settle ourselves in." She gave him a generous tip, and went through the door he held open for her. "Oh, how glad I am to be here. I suppose we could get at extra blankets? He—he's apt to be cold."

"Right in the linen closet, down the hall."

"We'll get them if we need them."

Sam deposited her bags in the room, opened the other doors, and then went down for the rest of the luggage. When he approached Room 17 with a handsome pigskin dressing case, he found the occupant sitting on the edge of the bed, bent over with his hands between his knees, and breathing hard. Sam's kind, freckled face was troubled.

"You all right?" he enquired, putting the case on the table.

"Yes. Fine. Call Sanderson, will you?"

Sam did so, and went downstairs. He had left the three golf bags belonging to the party leaning against the counter; he put them in the lobby chest, and was just emerging when the office telephone rang. He went back to answer it, and heard Sanderson's voice:

"That you, Sam? Hang on a minute."

"Yes, sir."

Sanderson's voice went on, to somebody else: "All right, Amby, you idiot. Go ahead, and make it short."

Sam said: "You want to make a call, Mr. Cowden?"

"Yes, I do. It's to Seal Cove. You know where that is?"

"Yes. Oakport exchange."

"I don't know the number, it's that summer theatre—'The Old Pier Players.'"

"I'll get the Oakport operator."

Sam got into communication with Oakport. Presently he said: "They have no telephone up there, Mr. Cowden."

"What? There must be one. That's crazy."

"No, sir, they haven't. No number listed."

"Perhaps they're all asleep. Ring them again."

"No number to ring."

"I don't understand. It's a theatre. They must have a telephone."

"Wait a minute." Sam again interviewed Oakport, and came back with the news: "They ain't installed yet. They only been there a week, and the poles was all down. There's been a lot of trouble with outlying districts since the storm last fall. Operator can get you Tucon."

"Where's that?"

"Little place on the back route from Oakport to Portland. They been getting their messages and telegrams left there in some store. Operator has the number. They might take your call, and ride down to the Cove with it."

"Oh, well; I hate to get them up, this time of night."

"It's only a little place. Might not anybody be around, late as this."

"I should think those people at the Cove would be wild."

"I should, too."

"Well, it's not so important as all that. I guess—"

Sanderson's voice said: "Amby, you are a jackass. I'll get him for you first thing in the morning. Now will you quit? I want to go to bed. I'm all in."

"I see now why there wasn't any message for me to-night."

"Of course. He couldn't get through. Quit, will you?"

"All right, Sam."

The receiver clicked. Sam exchanged some words with Oakport, and returned to his magazine. He was deep in it, when a curious sound on the stairs beside him made him look up, and then stare, transfixed. The sound had been, as he thought, laboured breathing.

He gazed incredulously at the pallid, smiling face, the tweed coat, the white silk muffler, the thick yellow chamois gloves, and the Panama hat; and he spoke as he had never before spoken to a guest of the Ocean House:

"What you doing down here?"

"Oh, you're there, are you? I wasn't sure you would be."

"Certainly I'm here."

"I thought you might be making your rounds. You do, don't you?"

"Yes, I do. You ain't going out, Mr. Cowden?"

"Not if you'll do something for me. I dropped my cigarette case. I had it in the car, and I know just where it must be—right outside, near the steps. It must have fallen out of my coat when Hugh Sanderson was helping me down."

Sam, remembering that awkward exit from the front seat, was not surprised to hear that something had been dropped in the process; but he continued to stare.

"Why didn't you telephone down?" he demanded. "Why didn't you send—"

"Sanderson's dead on his feet; I'm as fresh as a daisy. I had two solid hours in bed, at Portsmouth."

"You could have telephoned."

"They're not asleep, yet. They might have heard me. I want my cigarette case; it's a good one."

"You were going poking out in this fog, lookin' for it? You must be crazy. You turn right round and go on back up to bed. I'll find it, if it's there." Sam got up, and produced a big torch from under the counter.

"All right. Keep your hair on. You can stick it in a drawer, till morning."

"I'd put it in the safe, only the safe's locked."

"Just stick it in a drawer."

"You go on up to bed. Your aunt will be crazy," said Sam, unconsciously using the tone that he would have employed for a bad boy, rather than a young man who had just come of age. He refused the dollar that was offered him over the banisters.

"I haven't found it yet," he said. "To-morrow will do." He went out, poked for some time about the roadway and the steps, and finally saw a grey, softly gleaming object in the rough grass that edged the drive. He turned it over, wondered at its subtle sheen, and went back into the hotel.

Relieved to see that the pale young man had disappeared, he went into the back office and bestowed the cigarette case in an envelope, and marked it. Then he shut the envelope carefully into a desk drawer. When he emerged, Gamadge was sliding a thick letter into the mail slot.

"See young Cowden?" asked Sam.

"No. What do you mean? Didn't they come long ago?"

"Sure they did." Sam glanced up at the clock, which said 1:40. "Half an hour. He came down again, just now."

"Shouldn't think they'd let him do that."

Sam explained. "I thought there was something funny about it," he said, looking bothered.

"How funny?"

"Can't exactly say. He was all bundled up."

"Well—he meant to go out in the fog, if you weren't here."

"He looked to me like he was goin' somewhere more than that."

"Where on earth should he be going, at this hour? And in his condition?"

"If he wasn't a sick feller, I'd have said he was goin' out to keep a date."

"Date! You must be dreaming. He doesn't know a soul in the place, so far as I can make out, except the Barclays."

"Well, I guess I am crazy; but he looked too much dressed up to be going out just to look for a cigarette case."

"Perhaps that heart trouble of his makes him cold. I think I've heard so." Gamadge turned towards the stairs and paused on the lowest step. "Come to think of it, Sam, it's his birthday."

"So he said."

"And it meant something to him, let me tell you! He's been a rich man for forty minutes."

Gamadge climbed to the first floor, and stood looking down the hall. Sam's story had impressed him; but he was inclined to think that they were both making too much of it.

"Hang it all," he thought, irresolute, his eyes wandering from one end of the silent corridor to the other. "I can't go knocking them up; they'd hear me, if I even scratched on his door. They must be down at that end—all the transoms are open. Shall I go back and get his room number from Sam? It does seem such a nursemaidy, rocking-chair thing to do. No, I won't. Nothing to it."

Gamadge, in fact, had a virtue that sometimes transformed itself into a fault; that of minding his own business. He went up to the second flight of stairs, into cold, fog-laden air; entered his room; and was in bed and asleep in ten minutes.

CHAPTER THREE

Not Much of a Birthday

A VIOLENT KNOCKING finally persuaded Gamadge to open his eyes. The room was flooded with sunshine. "All right, all right," he muttered.

Waldo, the tall bellboy, put his head around the door. "I forgot to call, Mr. Gamadge. It's nearly nine."

"Good Lord, Macpherson will be raging." Gamadge sat up annoyed. "What's the idea, forgetting your calls?"

"We're all upset. It don't matter about Mr. Macpherson, he's down at the cliff."

"Where?"

"Down the road, on the lookout. Something terrible happened. One of the guests fell off the rocks."

"That's too bad. When? This morning?"

"Last night. Young feller that just checked in. Name's Cowden."

"Cowden!" Gamadge suddenly came awake. "Yes, sir. They think he had a heart attack, and fell over the cliff. Everybody's down there. They just took the remains away."

Gamadge, staring at the bellboy, swung one leg over the side of the bed. "What did he go down there for?"

"They don't know."

"Do they know when it happened?"

"Somebody said around two o'clock."

Gamadge groaned. "Who found him?"

"One of the gypsies from the camp down in the grove. Kid named Stanley. He was out on the beach early, about seven, picking up driftwood and jelly seaweed before the beach cleaners got around. The body had a typewritten name and address pinned inside the coat; case of accidents."

"Of course. So somebody telephoned here?"

"They got hold of Mr. Sanderson—he's a feller came with the Cowden party. He went and got the Barclays—they're some relation of the feller that got killed. The sheriff sent a detective over, and he's grilling Sam Leavitt."

"I didn't know the sheriff had a detective."

"Some friend of his; state detective, or something. He wants to see you, Mr. Gamadge; that's how I remembered about your call."

"Thanks very much." Gamadge swung the other leg to the floor. "Where is he?"

"Room 17—that's the room the Cowden feller had."

"You tell him I'll be there as soon as I've had a swallow of coffee. Tell him I want to be grilled, too."

Waldo rushed away. Gamadge had a quick bath, pulled on his clothes, and went down to the dining room. At 9:40 he knocked at the door of Number 17.

"Come in," said a mild, slow voice. Gamadge entered, closed the door behind him, and looked down into the square face of a grey, stocky man who sat in a hard rocking chair. He wore a business suit, waistcoat and all, and black, shiny shoes. Sam was perched on a hard chair opposite him. He looked puzzled and upset, and he evidently needed sleep; otherwise, his grilling did not seem to have had serious effects on him.

"Mr. Gamadge," he exclaimed, "ain't this awful?"

"Yes, it is."

"You just missed him. If you'd seen him, you might have felt the way I did, and gone after him, or something."

"I might have." He nodded to the grey man, who nodded in return. "I'm Mitchell," he said.

"How do you do?" Gamadge's eyes wandered around the small, neat room, which showed no signs of occupancy except a dressing gown and a pair of pyjamas lying on the bed, a closed suitcase on the floor, and a closed pigskin dressing case on the table. "Did they pull you out of bed, Sam?" he asked.

"No; I hadn't gone to bed. I don't get relieved till 7:30."

"First-class witness, Leavitt is," said Mitchell. "Mr. Gamadge: What about this cocoa?"

"Cocoa." Gamadge's eyes roved about the room again, and came back to Mitchell. "Cocoa?" he asked, with polite blankness.

"Sam Leavitt tells me the deceased had cocoa at Colonel Barclay's cottage last night, and was sick afterwards."

"Mis' Cowden said so. She said he was sick coming up here in the car, an' it must have been the cocoa."

"I remember, now. Young Cowden and his sister had cocoa. The rest of us were accommodated with whisky."

"His sister had some, did she?" Mitchell looked at Sam. "Did it disagree with her, too?"

"Not as far as I could see. She was spry enough. Grabbed her little suitcase, jumped out of the car, and skipped right up the steps and into the lobby. She wasn't sick."

"How'd the boy act? Didn't seem to be in pain, or anything?"

"He was fine, once the other feller got him out of the car. I thought first he was kind of weak, and I whistled Kimball up from the garage, so the feller wouldn't have to leave him. But afterwards you wouldn't have known he was sick, if it hadn't been for his colour, and his hard breathin'. He come over to the desk, and looked up at the clock, and started jokin' about it bein' his birthday. Lively as anybody."

"Well, thanks, Sam. That's all for now. You go on to bed."

Sam went; Gamadge sat down on the chair he had vacated, and lighted a cigarette. When he looked up, Mitchell's small blue eyes were on him.

"You know any of these people well, Mr. Gamadge?" he asked.

"I met the Cowdens last night, for the first time. The Barclays I know as summer acquaintances." He added, "I don't think there was anything the matter with their cocoa, Mitchell. I don't think Mrs. Cowden meant that there was."

"The boy being tired, and sick, anyway, it might have upset him. That the idea?"

"I think that was the idea."

"Of course we have to have an inquest." Mitchell spread out his hands, and contemplated his square fingers.

"I suppose you do."

"Our medical examiner seems to think that the deceased died of this heart trouble he had."

"And fell off the cliff during the attack?"

"Yes. We'd like to get hold of some kind of a working theory about why he went down there, in his condition, at that time of night."

"That cigarette-case business certainly points to a planned affair."

"I don't think there's any doubt but what it was. There seems to be some idea in the family that he was going for good."

"Really? Going where?"

"Up to a place called Seal Cove, where they have a summer theatre. He has a cousin up there."

"So he told me. He was interested in the place. But—"

"Sanderson tells me he was planning to go up to-day. You know he was having his twenty-first birthday?"

"Yes; I heard about that."

"All of it?"

"If you mean the financial situation, the Barclays told me about it last night."

"Not much of a birthday," said Mitchell, again spreading his hands and examining the fingers.

"And he was looking forward to it, too."

"Was, was he?"

"All kinds of plans. He was going to sign his will, to-day."

"It's missing."

"Is it, really? He put it in his pocket—I saw him; if that was the document he showed Fred Barclay."

"If it ain't there," Mitchell jerked his head towards the pigskin dressing case; "it ain't anywhere."

"How very odd."

"You'd think he'd take a thing like that case with him, if he was going off for good."

"He wouldn't have been able to carry anything, Mitchell. I know he'd never think of such a thing. But if he was going off for good, and didn't want his family to know it, why did he struggle through that cigarette-case comedy with Sam, instead of quietly decamping by way of the fire escape? It's only one flight down, and the dining room and kitchens are at that end of the hotel. Not a soul would have seen him."

"He might not have known about the fire escape; and even if he did, he had a good reason for not going that way. He'd have had to pass his tutor's room, his sister's room, and his aunt's room; and even if they were in bed, the transoms were open."

"They were; I saw them."

"And those people hadn't hardly time to get to bed, much less to sleep. One squeak out of his shoes, or anything like that, and the trip was off."

"So it was."

"I'm going into all this, Mr. Gamadge, for two reasons. First, they think this cousin of his, Atwood, must have planned to drive down from the Cove, last night, and meet him at the cliff, and take him up there to that summer theatre. 'The Old Pier Players'; that's what the name is. Now, this Atwood hasn't come forward; so I'm going up there to see him. If there was any kind of an accident, down on the rocks, he may not want to admit being there; but we found a folding cheque book in the boy's pocket, and one of the cheques in it was made out to Atwood, and signed. Made out for one hundred dollars. It was folded right back with the others, and anybody going through his pockets would be likely to miss it. Now, Colonel Barclay tells me you're interested in handwriting, and ink, and so on, Mr. Gamadge."

"I am; trouble is, the handwriting and ink I'm interested in is usually from one to two hundred years old."

"Don't say!" Mitchell looked disappointed. "My idea was that perhaps you could tell whether that cheque was made out last night. If it was, you could argue that the deceased meant to *give* it to Atwood, last night."

"You could." Gamadge looked round at the immaculate blotter on the desk, and the brand-new steel pen. Mitchell said:

"There ain't a mark on that blotter, and no other blotter was in the room. He had a fountain pen—empty."

"Oh. Well, Mitchell, there's a faint, feeble possibility that I could tell you whether the ink on that cheque is Ocean House ink."

Mitchell's eye lighted.

"Don't count on it. If I can, it will be a lucky break. And I have no materials here to work with."

"I'll get 'em for you from Portland. The other request I have to make is this: You saw all these people, Mr. Gamadge; and you're the only person outside the family, except Sam, that did see 'em. I'd like to hear what you thought of 'em."

"That's a long order, on such a short acquaintance, I can tell you more or less what I thought of the boy himself; he was very attractive."

Mitchell raised his eyebrows. "Sam says he looked like a livin' corpse."

"His colour was startling, but otherwise he had a very attractive personality. His illness had warped him, I suppose; he was obviously spoiled; selfish, perhaps; self-indulgent; a trifle too used to having all the money in the outfit. But he had character. His illness hadn't made him morbid, he wasn't peevish, and he had (as you know already) physical and moral courage. I should say he was affectionate and generous to people he liked; and I should say he liked a good many people. I liked him, Mitchell. I hoped he'd get a little fun out of his money."

There was a pause. Then Mitchell said, woodenly: "Sheriff doesn't like the job of asking these bereaved ladies questions."

"No; very unpleasant. So he passed the buck to you."

"I don't like it any better than he does."

"What questions do you want to ask them, anyway?"

Mitchell glanced at him, glanced out of the window, and said: "There'll be a post mortem."

"Naturally."

"What's more, there's a Doctor Ethelbert Baines in the hotel, and they say he's a big man in New York."

"He is. A very big man."

"He's a friend of the Cowdens. He's going over to the Centre to check up on Cogswell's findings."

"You couldn't have a better opinion."

"He had to die sometime soon, they tell me," continued Mitchell. "Nothing specially funny about his dying last night, after all he'd been through yesterday. He had a bad attack at Portsmouth."

Gamadge surveyed him for some moments in silence. Then, smiling faintly, he leaned back in his chair, stretched out his legs, gazed at the ceiling, and said reflectively; "What if they find some ante-mortem bruises? Or what if they don't? Having some imagination, it worries you a little to consider how soon he died after coming into his money. You can't help realising that if he had lived only a short time longer, he would have been living among new friends, spending his fortune on them, perhaps even getting married. You reflect morosely on the fact that his sister is his sole heir, since he doesn't seem to have got that will signed and witnessed. Is she his sole heir, Mitchell?"

"Yes, she is. But I don't—"

"You don't feel like going into the next room and asking her if she pushed her brother off the cliff, last night. That would certainly have given him a fatal heart attack, wouldn't it?"

Mitchell gave him a doubtful and grudging look. "I haven't said any such thing."

"So I had to say it for you. You want me to introduce you to these ladies?"

"I have to go easy."

"Certainly. The approach will have to be indirect."

"You mean you'll do it?"

"Certainly I'll do it. Why not?" Gamadge turned, and was about to pick up the telephone.

"Look out!" Mitchell started forward. "I have some finger-print men coming down this afternoon."

"Oh." Gamadge picked the receiver up by its edge. "That you, Wilks? Give me—no, wait a minute. Send one of the boys up, will you?" He said over his shoulder: "Mrs. Cowden may not be answering her telephone."

"In a hurry, ain't you?" Mitchell studied him curiously, as he replaced the receiver on its hook.

"Aren't you?"

"I have to see Mrs. Barclay, and get up to the Cove."

"I'll drive you up, if you're agreeable. I'd like to see the place. The poor little beggar asked me to go. I think I'd do well to accept his invitation."

Peabody, the short bellboy, knocked and came in.

"Oh, Peabody," said Gamadge. "Go to Mrs. Cowden's door, will you, and ask her if she will speak to Mr. Gamadge on the telephone."

"Yes, sir."

"If she says she doesn't know who I am, tell her I'm a friend of the Barclays. She met me there last night."

Peabody walked solemnly down the hall, past the intervening room, to Number 21. They heard his knock, and a low-voiced conversation. He returned, his solemn face lighted by an unaccustomed smile. "She says yes."

"I don't believe that everybody could have got me that interview, Peabody. I'll remember it. Now go down and tell Wilks to put me on to Room 21. Tell him it's all right, Mrs. Cowden expects the call."

Peabody left, and Gamadge waited for a few moments, and then lifted the receiver again.

"Mrs. Cowden? I apologise for bothering you at such a time. First, let me ask if I can be of any help. Anything at all... Yes, I thought they might be at the Centre; that's why I... Let me know if there's anything, then. How is Miss Cowden?... Oh, I'm very sorry... You got hold of Baines? Good. I was going to say I could probably find him for you, on the golf course... Peabody did? That boy's a jewel.

"What I called up about, there's a man here from the sheriff's office, quite a nice fellow, state detective. He wants some data; you know these formalities. He didn't feel that he could bother you this morning, but I had an idea you might be willing to help him out. Of course he could wait for Colonel Barclay to get back from the Centre... You'll see him? I was pretty sure you would. Shall I get hold of him, then, and bring him up, say in half an hour? I agree with you—much better to get these things over with... Not at all, I'm only too glad. Good-bye."

Gamadge replaced the receiver gently on its hook, and turned to Mitchell with a condescending bow. Mitchell's answering look held a mild and questioning wonder.

"What's the matter?" asked Gamadge.

"You're a cool customer." Mitchell was amused. He went on, frowning: "Did she say Miss Cowden was sick?"

"Collapsed. They had Baines see to her."

"Now, that's too bad. I was counting on seeing her."

"You may, yet; who knows?"

Somebody knocked, and little Peabody made a second appearance, holding a large manila envelope as if it were a tea tray.

"State policeman just brought it," he said, and backed out, more solemn than ever. Mitchell said: "I will say they were pretty quick, over there. Not so bad, for the Centre." He took out a photograph, glanced at it, handed it to Gamadge, and busied himself with a typewritten report.

The picture showed a figure that looked merely like garments, carelessly flung down, so insignificant was it, spread-eagled below towering rocks. A Panama hat lay near it, and its tweed topcoat was twisted away from one shoulder, as if torn off in the fall. The body lay face down; there were no injuries to be seen on the back of the head; but the upper half of the face was a black smear.

Gamadge looked at it, turned it this way and that, and studied it from all angles. Then he handed it to Mitchell.

"Take it away," he said. "I don't like it."

"You can imagine how the little feller that found it felt. Those gypsies are hard-boiled characters, even the children; but when he got hold of the beach cleaners, this Stanley boy was crying."

"I feel like crying myself."

"Here's the list of what young Cowden had in his pockets. No papers, except that cheque book, and a bill or two. They sent the cheque book; here it is."

"Must I handle it by the edges, too?"

"No, I got that printed. No prints on it but his."

Gamadge opened it, and unfolded the signed cheque, which had not been torn out; unless opened, it resembled all the blank ones. He studied it, while Mitchell continued:

"No driving licence, of course. A wallet with some stamps and thirty-four dollars in cash. Handkerchief. Pair of chamois gloves, rolled up. Little bottle of medicine—iodide of potassium. He had a wrist watch on, unbreakable glass, but it was under him, and it was smashed. Stopped at 2.9."

"Which is when he died?"

"Far as anybody can tell. He was out in the cold and wet for all those hours. The spray reaches that place, when the tide's high. It was going out at two, but it was still high enough to soak him. Then there was his physical condition, and nothing solid in his stomach since he had dinner at Portsmouth. Two-nine suits the medical examiner all right."

Mitchell replaced the list in the envelope, added the photograph, rose, and approached the table. He opened the lid of the pigskin dressing case, and then paused to wind a handkerchief around his right hand. A multitude of glass and silver objects winked against a rich dark-green silk lining; Gamadge came up to watch, while Mitchell began carefully to remove them one by one. They were so cunningly fitted that it was a task of some delicacy to get them out of their individual nests.

"Quite a bag," remarked Gamadge.

"How much would you say a thing like this was worth?" asked Mitchell.

"I hardly know. Where does it come from?"

Mitchell turned a flat tooth-paste container upside down, and said: "Tomlinson, Piccadilly."

"Where the good bags come from. Say five hundred dollars."

"My goodness."

"Did you see the famous cigarette case? That might have cost almost as much."

"The young feller didn't stint himself."

"He had so few toys, Mitchell. My own little car cost more than that bag, and nobody thinks it was an extravagance. He couldn't drive a car."

"You certainly liked that boy."

"I was dammed sorry for him. He must have known that it was to everybody's interest to keep him going until he was twenty-one."

"That's putting it strong. You might say, if you wanted to talk like that, that it was to his sister's interest to have him die as soon afterwards as possible."

"And to the interest of all the people benefiting by that will you're hunting for."

Mitchell took out a glittering toothbrush case. "He never even took his toothbrush. Well, that's all there is in the bag, far as I can see. Don't these things—" He felt around the bottom edges of the lining, seized a tiny loop of ribbon, and pulled. "Not much secret about this."

"Only a compartment for valuables." Gamadge craned to look. "One pair of platinum cuff links, pearl evening studs, old-fashioned tiepin, probably his father's."

"He don't seem to have set much value on his things." Mitchell began to replace the fittings, and had just finished when somebody knocked.

"Who's there?" he demanded, hastily forcing the last objects into their places, and closing the lid.

"Sanderson."

"Come right in, Mr. Sanderson. I was waiting for you."